BLACK WATER

LUCAS PEDERSON

SEVERED PRESS
HOBART TASMANIA

BLACK WATER

Copyright © 2020 by Lucas Pederson

WWW.SEVEREDPRESS.COM

ISBN: 978-1-922323-65-1

Dedicated to my lovely daughter, Mary. Your monster, your story. Love you.

THE GULF OF MEXICO: 2022

Carlito Guerra frowned, placed the muzzle of his pistol on Max's sweaty forehead and pulled the trigger.

His people quickly disposed of the body.

After a moment of reflection, Carlito tapped a spot on the map with a well-manicured finger. "Hay tuneles aqui?"

Brent nodded, forcing himself not to look at all the blood splattered everywhere on the plastic covered floor and desk from poor Max. "Yes. An entire system of tunnels. Huge." He waited for the translator, nodded and continued. "I think we should tap into them." He waited a few seconds, then proceeded. "With the border shutdown, this could be a goldmine for you."

Such was the life of being an American on the coast of Mexico. Brent had been traveling here for so long, though, he almost knew every word before the translator could relay the message. Though, not always.

He leaned forward and ran a finger along a stretch of tunnel his people pinged. A direct route. Poor Max be damned. Guy shouldn't have been so pushy. Especially with the likes of Carlito Guerra.

"This is the closest one," Brent said and waited for the translator. "Leads directly to Freeport, Texas." Brent double tapped a smaller, though much longer tributary. "Brownville, Texas or St. Petersburg, Florida would be the best unsuspecting route, though." Brent grinned. "No one expects undersea tunnels, either way."

Mr. Guerra nodded while the translator spoke. Eventually, he sighed, leaned back in his chair, and lit a cigarette. As though on cue, a tall man emerged from the shadows and carefully placed a black briefcase on the desk.

"Brownsville, Texas," Guerra said. "Asegúrate de que el camino esté despejado cuando llame."

The translator said, "Brownsville, Texas. Make sure the way is clear when I call."

Brent opened the briefcase, smiled, closed it. "The way will be clear, amigo. We'll be prepared."

The translator did her thing. Guerra nodded and blew a jet of silvery-blue smoke, grinned and waved a hand, dismissing Brent.

Such was the way of Carlito Guerra, leader of the Gulf Cartel. Or rather, the Cartel Del Golfo, if you wanted to get all authentic about it.

Brent, however, didn't give a shit.

All that mattered was the money.

For now, anyway…

He stood, gave Guerra a respectful nod, turned and made his way toward the door.

"Esperar."

Brent's hand fell away from the golden doorknob. He knew what that word meant in Spanish.

Wait.

Not a good sign. His other hand crept to the inside of his blue blazer where his forty-five hung from a shoulder holster. He did not turn around, heart stuttering.

"Yes, Señor Guerra. Is there something more?"

The drug lord's translator rattled off what Brent said.

A few seconds later, the whisper of handmade leather loafers over polished tile floated to his ears. Brent's breathing paused. His hand curled around the butt of the forty-five.

Directly behind him, Guerra said, "Olvidaste esto, amigo."

The translator said, "You forgot this, friend."

Brent's hand fell away from the gun and he turned around. Guerra smiled. His brown eyes held Brent's gray ones. Then the man held up Brent's passport. He waggled it there between them for a moment, then tossed it at Brent's chest. How the leader of the Gulf Cartel got ahold of it, Brent didn't know.

Carlito Guerra flicked that dismissive hand at Brent again and turned back toward his desk. "Espero que no haya problemas. Porque, si hay…"

"I expect there will be no problems. Because, if there are…" the translator said.

Brent nodded, trying not to let his fear show, even to the woman translator eyeing him carefully. "Yes, sir." He spun, opened the door and left the room as casually as his sparking nerves would allow.

He didn't fully relax until he was on a plane to Austin, Texas.

Even then, he wondered who would be watching him…

TWO YEARS LATER

CHAPTER 1

"Get down!" Andy shoved Sergeant Genson to the ground and drew his sidearm.

He moved forward, aiming the pistol at the shadow down the hall. The overhead lights flickered, not quite revealing the thing's identity. Andy's heart thundered. A bead of sweat trickled down the side of his face.

A storm howled around the old factory outside.

The thing at the end of the hall moved. And it was a thing. Not a man or woman, but some dark creature. Maybe a wolf, but it appeared to be too big. Too broad. Too—

"The hell ya doin', Miller?" Genson said and stepped next to Andy. "That thing ain't got a gun, ya know?"

Andy's lips pressed together in a thin line. Yeah. He knew. Might've overreacted a bit with shoving his commanding officer to the ground and all. But, still, he had to show the older guy he knew how to control a situation. The tension in the air dissipated a bit.

Genson grunted. "Can't tell what the hell it is. Can you?"

"No," Andy said, watching the shadowy creature pace back and forth. "Can you shine a flashlight on it?"

He felt more than saw Genson's withering look. Like acid eating away the side of his face.

Even so, the older man brought out a flashlight and pointed it at the pacing creature at the end of the hall. Then he let out a long breath too heavy to be a sigh. More like a whoosh or a gut punch.

Andy's heart stopped for a beat or two. Indeed, the entire world seemed to pause for a bit. His eyes widened. "Is that a—a—"

"Don't move, kid," Genson whispered. "Keep your voice down. And for the love of God, do *not* shoot at it."

"Werewolf," Andy whispered.

Genson grunted. "Fairytales, boy. That's a coyter. Part tiger, part wolf, ya know."

Andy blinked. "They're real?"

"Yup. God knows how many are just crawlin' around out there at night." Genson's flashlight lowered to a quivering body. Blood pumped from an open throat and pooled around him. "It got our perp, though."

"Lovely," Andy said, grimacing. He fought the urge to vomit. Just barely.

"Nasty bastards, aren't they?" Genson drew his own sidearm. A Desert Eagle 50. Not at all regulation, nor near it. Way too powerful.

But, then again, they weren't exactly cops either…

"Want ya to take a knee," Genson said. "This bastard won't let us outta here alive. Coyters got bad tempers."

Andy did as his partner told him to. He took a knee, keeping his aim on the coyter.

"If I miss," Genson whispered, "unload on the bastard until I get another shot off. Their bone density is a lot stronger than ours and hide like an elephant. Aim for the head."

The elephant hide thing was a myth, Andy knew from research on the creatures that were supposed to all be dead by now. Creatures spliced and bred in a lab and escaped to reign terror on half the country before finally being eradicated. Or so he thought. Somehow, the extermination crews missed one…

It hissed and growled, baring long fangs that might as well belong to a saber-toothed tiger. Its amber eyes flared with every flicker of the light. An unnerving sight, especially since it was mainly humans Andy was used to taking down this late at night. Still, he tried to exert control. Genson looked for that kind of thing, or so the guys in the locker room told him. He knew locker room talk was mainly bullshit but couldn't help but believe that tid-bit about Sergeant Genson. The older man wanted a partner who could control a situation.

Andy wanted to be on the Elite Patrol, after all. It would bring in the income he needed for his family. Or, rather, his kids. His wife, Audra, took off on them last May. Hadn't heard from her since. Which pissed him off because he couldn't divorce her if he couldn't find her. All that mattered right now were his beautiful kids. With both edging into their teens, though, they asked all too often why he was gone so much.

They weren't allowed to know, though.

Safer they didn't know.

The coyter lowered its vulpine head, amber eyes fixed on the two men.

"Steady," Genson whispered. "Steady, now."

A growl rumbled from down the hall. Even with the storm raging outside, Andy heard it.

Taking down creatures wasn't in his job description, though one of the many hazards. As Genson once put it, "Bastards everywhere, kid. Most of 'em human. Some not. Just gotta roll with the punches and claws, ya know?"

He leveled his forty-five on the coyter and waited for Genson.

And waited some more.

Andy was about to give the older man a nudge, or something, when the older man fired the Desert Eagle. The loud report in the narrow office hallway made Andy's ears ring. He winced, pain shooting through his head like a sharp, steel spike.

Genson's shot struck the coyter in the right flank just as it turned to continue pacing. It yelped, staggered, fell, and before Andy's brain caught up, the beast sprinted at them.

All long fangs and fiery rage.

"Shoot it," Genson shouted, still pointing the Desert Eagle at the creature.

Andy squeezed off three shots.

All but one went wild. The third disintegrated an ear. It yelped again, crashed into a wall, shook its head, and glowered at the men with its glowing, amber eyes. Drool clung from its dark, furry chin.

"Shoot it," Genson said, but Andy froze. That amber glare held him in sway.

It scrambled in its own blood and shot forward toward Andy. The air leaked out of his lungs and he knew what was going to happen. Because he couldn't move, let alone shoot his gun, they'd both be torn to ribbons. The scene played out, in all its gory detail, in his mind and—

"Goddamn it, kid," Genson said and blew a large hole in the coyter's head.

It collapsed and skidded along the grimy floor, leaving a trail of blood in its wake.

The coyter's muzzle pressed against Genson's boots and didn't move. A long breath whooshed out of its mouth where more blood poured out.

Genson humphed, stepped back and said, "Gonna need new boots."

Andy, stuck in a state of awe, only gaped at the dead beast. There was little else he could do until Genson grabbed his arm and yanked him to his feet.

"Shoot till you're outta bullets or it's dead," Genson said, voice like a growl. "Told ya that enough times over the months ya think it'd sink in."

Andy opened his mouth, closed it. His heart was still a thunderous mess in his chest.

Genson's glare softened. He sighed and patted Andy's back. "Let's get Napoli and his team in here to clean this all up, eh?"

Genson limped toward the dead perp. The one they tracked from a tunnel under the old border almost twenty miles away. A long trek for a perp. But Genson was convinced the man was part of the Cartel. Perhaps even a drug lord.

Andy's gaze drifted from his commanding officer to the dead coyter on the floor and wondered, not for the first time, why he chose such a crazy job. He could've played it safe and been a mechanical engineer. He had all the schooling to launch a viable career. But, in the end, he decided he needed more out of a career. He needed to be making a difference. And if that difference benefitted humankind by taking down drug runners and sex traffickers, then so be it.

But he fucked up this time. Not the first time, but enough for Genson to yell at him. Genson hadn't yelled at him for at least two months. Now...God, it was like he was green again. Until tonight, he thought he was doing pretty good. Green. New to the job. That's exactly how Andy felt while he stared at the dead coyter.

"Hey," Genson shouted from down the hall. "Get a medevac here." Genson knelt beside the perp and placed a hand over the gouged throat.

Andy sighed. He didn't have the heart to tell Genson the man couldn't be saved. He'd lost too much blood and the damage the coyter made to his throat appeared to be beyond repair.

Andy pressed his throat mic and radioed for a clean-up crew and a medevac.

Heart thrumming, his gaze returned to the dead coyter and there he stood until help arrived.

***

Genson stood, hands on his hips. A stony expression blanketed his face while the medics secured a sheet over the dead perp and lifted the corpse onto a gurney.

Andy kept his distance, not sure what to do or say. Hell, what was he *supposed* to do or say anyway? The perp was dead. The coyter was dead. Case closed. Well, for now, at least. There would be a new case. There was always a new case.

All of that didn't take away the shame wriggling into his gut, though. He wished it had. To be entirely free of uncertainty would be enough. But it didn't. Anyone else probably wouldn't be so worried, but he still wanted into the Elite Patrol, so he needed to get his shit together.

That's if it wasn't too late...

Once the perp was loaded up and the helicopter departed, Genson turned to Andy. The older man's stony gray eyes held horrors within them the likes Andy had yet to see. A haunted man.

For the longest time, Genson and Andy stared at each other until, finally, the older man sighed and lowered his gaze.

"Let's get back to our post, kid."

Andy opened his mouth, not sure what to say, but feeling like he should say *something*, but Genson shook his head. Andy shut his mouth and looked away.

Strong hands gently gripped his shoulders, surprising Andy. He didn't even hear Genson move. He frowned at the older man whose eyes were not stony at all now.

"This is how we learn, kid," Genson said. "Mistakes. You got what it takes. Just gotta believe in yourself." He paused, frowned. "No. *Trust* yourself. That's the main thing. Trust in yourself."

He backed away, leaving Andy gaping and once again at a loss for words.

Genson chuckled, clapped Andy's shoulder and pointed to another helicopter waiting a few yards from the office building where they confronted the coyter. The outside of the dilapidated building was just as creepy as the inside. The last few acrid raindrops pattered onto Andy's helmet and shoulders. The storm passed through, as all storms did, leaving the region sucking up all the moisture it could before morning arrived and the sun scorched the hell out of that part of the world before moving onto the next.

That time of year and all.

They made their way to the helicopter and strapped in.

Andy wanted to tell Genson he was sorry. He wanted to say he fucked up and would do better next time.

But, in the end, he stared out the side window of the helicopter and fell into deep silence.

Because, really…there was nothing to say.

He messed up.

That was that.

CHAPTER 2

Post 143 wasn't much. "Nothin' but some plywood and spacklin'," Genson liked to say. But it did its job sheltering them from the elements and wildlife.

Well, almost all the wildlife.

There were a few times Andy woke up for his shift, nights, to find a scorpion or rattlesnake hanging out beside his cot.

"Critters always find a way," Genson was also fond of saying.

Easy for him to say, Andy thought now while easing his weary body into bed. *He's not the one waking up to venomous visitors every other night.*

Genson was outside somewhere. Probably patrolling instead of in the crow's nest scouting for runners. The man liked to be right in the thick of things, unlike Andy, who'd rather have a plan and take down perps from a distance then gather them for questioning. Not Genson, though. The older man sought out conflict. He took down individual perps or in groups. Didn't matter.

Perhaps that was why he was one of the great Elites. The guy took on more than any one person should and always came out on top. How he did it, Andy couldn't be sure. The guy could only teach Andy so much before Andy's shift started. In fact, they interacted in passing, rather than sitting and actually talking or teaching lessons.

"Gotta always look for the out," Genson liked to tell Andy in passing. "Got a group of 'em? Don't let yourself get surrounded. Take 'em out quick one by one."

And when asked: "What if the groups of people aren't drug runners?" Genson grunted and shrugged. "Not our job to pick'n choose, kid. If they're innocent, that'll all come out in the wash during their trials. We just nab 'em and eliminate as necessary."

Not wanting to wedge a divide between him and the older man, Andy kept his mouth shut. He didn't agree with Genson at all on how to treat people who managed to get across the border. The patrols needed better equipment and more manpower to vet everyone. Most of all…they needed to quit making assumptions like Genson. Veteran Elite or not.

There needed to be middle ground.

With the weight of the recent battle against a coyter still sinking into him and the death of a perp, Andy somehow fell into a deep and dreamless sleep.

Sweet, cool darkness embraced him like an old lover.

***

Andy woke to Genson shaking him, which never happened.

"Bastards everywhere," Genson said, face smeared with grime and sweat. Eyes wild in their sockets. "Get the fuck up, kid. Gotta defend our post."

Andy sat up, rubbed sleep boogers from his eyes and frowned while Genson opened a gun locker and brought out one of the .50-cals. M2s, if one wanted to get technical. He hefted it and shot a wink at Andy.

"Got a bunch of 'em out there. You better grab the other one."

"Wait," Andy said and shook his head. "What's going on?"

"Ya deaf now?" Genson loaded the M2. "Get up and defend your country!"

Andy swung his legs over the edge of the cot, head throbbing with a dull ache. His bladder felt like it was about to burst.

Genson grabbed his arm and yanked him to his feet. Andy about pissed himself right there.

"We're surrounded, kid. I got us locked down and we can pick 'em off from the nest."

"Who?" Andy asked.

Genson shot Andy a withering look. "Who do ya think? Goddamn Cartel come to take us out, that's who. Now, gear up and meet me in the nest. Gonna be a long night."

The older man hurried out of the small bedroom and into the short hall leading to the stairs for the crow's nest. Andy blinked after him, not sure what to do. He never saw Genson so worked up. So...scared. The sight alone drove an icy spike into his gut.

Andy didn't exactly rush to get geared up or load his own M2. But he slung an M4 over his shoulder and headed for the crow's nest steps anyway. Because it was his duty. If he wanted to move up into the Elite, he needed to stop overthinking and just—

"Took ya long enough," Genson said, stepping out the shadows near the front doors. All the terror in his face and eyes had vanished. He was the solid, steely man Andy came to know from day one.

Andy turned fully to the older man. Confusion sank its claws into him. He glanced around before his gaze once more settled on Genson. "What's going on?"

The older man let a smile slip from his leathery face before sucking it back in again. "Something that's come to my attention and needs to be addressed."

Hand gripping his M4, Andy readied himself for an attack.

But Genson snorted and waggled a finger at him. "Oh, come now, kid. No need to get all excited. Not like I'm gonna—"

Genson lunged at Andy, knife blade glinting in the raw light of a sixty-watt bulb overhead. Andy leaped to the side and kidney punched Genson a couple of times before the older man spun around. The knife slashed through the chest of Andy's black tactical gear but didn't touch the skin. At least Andy didn't think so. No time to worry about it now.

He ducked, avoiding another slash. Didn't stop the knee that struck his shoulder, though, knocking him backward and off his feet. He dropped to the floor hard on his ass, and scrambled back before Genson could bury the knife in his eye. Andy lifted the M4, but Genson kicked it away and shifted to stab Andy.

Without thinking, Andy smacked the knife out the older man's hand and drew his own. He booted Genson in the right knee and the man dropped like a sack of potatoes. Genson growled and went for his sidearm.

Andy went for the killing blow.

Then Genson said, "Slower than molasses, kid. But good job."

If Andy had put any more force behind his boost, it wouldn't have mattered what Genson said. The older man would be flopping around like a beached fish with a knife buried in his throat.

Fortunately, Andy stumbled to the side and Genson caught him before he went crashing into a wall.

Heart bashing itself against the walls of his chest, Andy staggered a bit and leaned against the wall. "What the actual hell?" It was all he could think of to say.

Genson huffed out a breath. Not quite a snort or grunt. "Welcome to the Elite, kid."

Andy straightened and faced the man. "What?"

Genson waved a dismissive hand at him and yawned. "We'll chat about it later. I'm beat. Probably how ya got the upper hand on me."

"Wait," Andy said and shook his head. "I don't have to take any tests or go through special training? I thought—"

"Whaddya think bein' stationed in the asshole of the country for two years was supposed to be? A camping trip?" Genson yawned again, stretched his back and turned toward the sleeping quarters. "Go get 'em tiger. I'm gonna get some sleep. We'll chat more about it when it's my shift."

With that, he ducked through the doorway and closed the door.

Andy blinked, mind reeling in bewilderment.

Eventually, he made his way up the concrete steps to the crow's nest of Post 143 and readied himself for twelve hours of waiting and watching. The night vision scopes and goggles would play hell with his sight after a while, but it could be worse. He could be trying to spotlight every little sound.

The crow's nest was an eighty-foot tower with a flattop and short, concrete walls—which came to about the bottom of Andy's chest—surrounding it in case someone tried shooting at them from the ground. Every six feet and mounted into the walls were scopes he now switched to night vision. Overhead was a light roof to keep the sun from scorching a person alive.

Andy switched everything to night vision, placed his night goggles on a stand near the old metal chair installed to help with leg fatigue. Not that it got used very much.

He also opened a long box and brought out the SRS-A2 Covert sniper rifle. This scope he also made sure was set on night vision. The short rifle helped with mobility more than anything. Easier and more efficient than lugging around a full-sized sniper rifle if there were multiple targets.

Not that he'd really needed to, but, in theory, it was supposed to help just in case.

Andy made his rounds looking through each scope before returning to the main one pointed directly at the border fence. He swept it back and forth slowly. No signs of movement. All clear. As it was most nights. He didn't know about all the other sentry posts, but his saw little action. Certainly nothing like Genson often spouted about. Andy had yet to catch more than three actual runners in a three-month span. Indeed, the last four months, or so, were a bit unproductive. Only time it got remotely busy was when Genson somehow rooted out a runner or two like a hog finding truffles.

Once his first rounds were complete, he stood staring into the dark soup of the night.

Could it be true that he was an Elite Patrol Officer now? Or was Genson messing with him? The guy did and said weird things. Case in point...claiming the Cartel was besieging the post. What would the morning bring?

The question both exhilarated and terrified Andy.

The hours dragged on and the worries about his career shifted to worries of his kids. Mary and Cass were with a longtime family friend, but that didn't help much. He still worried about them. How they were doing in school.

What problems were they facing from day to day? It had been almost a year since he got to hug them and kiss the tops of their heads. God, he missed them so much. Every so often he was able to video chat with them, but it felt like they wanted to talk to him less and less. A fact he couldn't ignore and, as a single father, scared him to death. Worse than any murderous Cartel drug runner. It scared him that he might be losing his children in some capacity. They seemed to be drifting from him. A slow tear in his spirit growing wider.

He couldn't lose his children.

They were all he had.

Sometime into his sixth hour on shift, about to make his rounds, someone behind him said, "Welcome to the Elite."

A sharp pinprick on the back of his neck and...

He knew nothing at all.

CHAPTER 3

Andy woke in a small room lined with stainless steel polished to such a high shine they might as well have been mirrors.

At least the bed he laid in was comfy and the blanket over him warm.

Somewhere, a muffled beep sounded. But it was so far away, he just didn't care much. Andy rolled onto his side and faced another wall of highly polished steel.

Didn't matter. His muscles were weak. Like he just tried to run a triathlon and collapsed barely halfway through. Rubbery. Fluffy cotton filled his head. All he wanted was sleep. Hell, he *needed* sleep. And before he knew it, sleep stole over him once more until—

"Need ya to get up, kid," Genson said. "Shit hit the damn fan."

Andy groaned, tried rolling back over but couldn't find the strength.

"Kid, you—"

"He was injected with a higher does than required," a warm, soothing voice said. "Let him rest a bit. We have time."

Andy's eyelids slipped shut and the voices faded into a garbled mess before he, gradually, fell into a blessed pit of silence.

***

When he woke for the second time, Genson was snoring away on a nearby couch. Dust motes danced in a golden shaft of light cast through a grimy window. Genson lay sprawled on the couch in his boxers and nothing else. His mouth hung open and a runner of silvery drool slipped down the side of his chin while he snored at the ceiling.

In the soft sunlight, he didn't appear to be the hard, stony man Andy knew. Rather, he looked like someone's grandfather fast asleep on the couch while watching football or an old movie. He didn't just seem older, but old. The man he would have been if not for being one of the Elite. Or, at least Andy liked to imagine. Genson was a different breed of man than he was used to. A little on the strange and unnerving side too. And yet, under all that rough exterior, the older man seemed to care about things. The country and the people in it, mostly. Andy wasn't sure if the man had any family or not.

Andy sat up, rubbed sleep boogers from his eyes and glanced around the room for a sink. His mouth was so dry, it might as well have been lined with carpet. He swallowed and his throat made a loud click. There was no sink. The room's polished steel walls reflected his bewilderment and disappointment.

He got out of bed and cringed when his bare feet touched the cold, tiled floor. He made it a couple of steps before realizing he too was in his underwear.

"What the fu—"

The door swung open, bathing Andy in no-nonsense fluorescent lighting, and exposing him to the world.

A tall man with a shiny bald head and wearing silver rimmed glasses strode into the room. He stopped once he noticed Andy standing a couple of feet from the bed. Behind Andy, Genson continued to snore away. Which was weird because the older man woke to the sound of a pin drop most of the time.

"Ah," the tall bald man said. He was wearing a long white lab coat. In his right hand he held a thin tablet. "Thought you might be awake. How are you feeling, Mr. Gains?"

Andy cocked an eyebrow. "Fine. Who the hell are you?"

The man chuckled lightly, brought out a rolling stool from under a short counter and sat. "I'm your doctor for your time here." His gaze drifted across the room. "Master Sergeant Genson is already cleared but he refused to leave your side."

Andy glanced over his shoulder at the snoring man. "Yeah?"

"Indeed," the doctor said. "He was granted approval to stay until you woke up."

"Where's he going now that I'm awake?"

The doctor sighed, then shook his head. "General Hawkins has ordered an Honorable Discharge for the Master Sergeant."

Andy's heart skipped a beat. "And Genson accepted?"

The doctor nodded his shiny bald head, solemnly. "Indeed."

Andy sighed. "Where are my clothes?"

To this, the doctor perked up a bit. "You'll be getting new gear as soon as we're finished."

Andy frowned. "Finished with what?"

"Why," the doctor said, "your physical, of course. Can't have you out there with a hernia or something, right?"

"Out where?" Andy spread his arms out on either side. "What the hell is going on?"

The doctor stood, towering over Andy a good foot or so. Though not in a menacing way. The doctor smiled. "It appears you'll be joining a top-secret mission."

"What mission?"

"It's top-secret."

Andy frowned. "You don't know?"

"No," said the doctor. "Just that it's top-secret." He held up his stethoscope and leaned forward. "Now, just let me check and see—"

"Fuck off," Andy said, slapping the doctor's hand away. "I want to see official documents stating I need a physical."

"It's legit, kid," Genson muttered behind him.

Andy turned and found the older man slipping into a pair of pants. Not the black gear he was accustomed to seeing on Genson, but actual jeans.

"I'm too damn old, the bastards said. Lies, though."

"Sergeant," the doctor said, "I assure you—"

Genson waved a hand. "Yeah, yeah. We went over all that." He pulled a t-shirt on and looked at Andy. "They'll check ya over, kid. Then you'll be shipped off to wherever they need ya. Nothing as grand as 'top-secret mission'. They're just trying to control ya like they do everyone. Manipulation. That's what they do best. They—"

"Thank you, Sergeant," the doctor said and chuckled. "But I think I can take it from here. The boy is well. You may leave now."

Genson grunted, tied his shoes and rounded the bed to stand before the tall doctor. Or rather, below.

"I'm goin'. Could ya give us a minute, though, string bean?"

"Sergeant," the doctor began.

"Only take a minute," Genson said. "Have something I want to tell the kid."

The doctor opened his mouth, closed it, sighed and left the room.

Once they were alone, Genson turned to Andy. "I don't know where you'll be posted this time around, kid. They wouldn't tell me."

"Why were you discharged, though?" Andy asked.

The older man looked away. "They wouldn't tell me that either." His gaze returned to Andy. "Doesn't matter. What matters is what might happen with you. Something messed up is going on. They're desperate for some reason. Shit hit the fan somewhere and they need ya."

Andy frowned, and glanced toward the open doorway.

Genson followed his gaze, grunted. "They're always listenin', kid. Sure I'll get a firm talkin' to." Though his face appeared to dim. His eyes lowered a bit. Andy's heart stuttered, realizing this was the last time he'd ever see or talk to Genson.

Somehow, he knew that. And it terrified him. Genson was, by all accounts, his mentor.

"You need to keep your head about you, kid," Genson said. "Some of these people are weasels in disguise. Might seem fine'n'dandy, but they're vile. Trust me on that." Genson placed his hands on Andy's shoulders and squeezed gently. His steely eyes softened. "The weasels are easy to find if ya look. It's the snakes ya gotta be worried about." He smiled. "It was an honor training ya, kid. Best pupil I've had in a long time. Just—"

"Alright, pops," a giant officer decked out like a makeshift MP said from the doorway. "Time's up."

Genson's eyes widened. His hands squeezed Andy's shoulders harder. "Mind the snakes, kid. Mind 'em well."

Before he could say anything more, the huge guard yanked him away and shoved him out the doorway.

Andy gaped, trying to process everything Genson tried to warn him about before the tall doctor sauntered back into the room and shut the door.

"Now," the doctor said, smiling a smile that seemed too long...too...toothy. "Where were we, Mr. Gains?"

The door closed behind the doctor, shrouding the room in gloom once more.

Andy backed away, ready for a fight. Genson's warning of weasels and snakes spread through his mind like a wildfire. The way the doctor moved closer and closer, that lengthy smile appearing to widen impossibly in the dimness of the room.

A soft click, and lights flickered on. Standing by the door, hand lowering from the light switch, stood a woman in a black pantsuit. Her dark hair was short and styled with a gentle swoop of the bangs. Her smoky gray eyes regarded Andy with interest. A corner of her mouth twitched in an almost smile.

The doctor, looming over Andy, said, "Sit, Mr. Gains. We'll get the examination over quickly."

Andy had forgotten about the doctor and had no choice but to sit on the bed.

The doctor didn't lie, however. The examination lasted only a couple of minutes. Rather, it was more like the physical Andy had to do before trying his hand at football in school. Which he sucked at and never went back to. At least the tall, bald doctor didn't do the, "turn your head and cough", thing. With the woman in the room that would have been a bit strange.

Once the doctor was finished with the exam, he backed away and the woman in the pantsuit sauntered forward, arms crossed over her chest.

"Officer Gains," she said in a soothing voice. Almost a purr. The same voice he remembered when he woke up briefly before. "How are you feeling?"

"Confused," he said.

Again, the corner of her mouth twitched in an almost smile. "Is that so? About what?"

"Well," he said, "for one thing...why was I drugged?"

"We didn't want you getting aggressive upon first meeting. If our agent had made himself known in the crow's nest out of nowhere, how would you have reacted?"

He thought about it, then nodded. "Okay. Fine. But if you had called the post to let us know, we would've let you in."

She smiled for real this time. "Would you? I wonder…"

"We've done it before with supply drop-offs."

She nodded, still approaching the bed where he sat. Arms still crossed over her chest. "Is that so? Well, I do apologize then. However, we needed to move quickly and you being awake would lead to questions, as you are doing now and wasting precious time."

Andy frowned, remembering her voice from when he first woke up. Her telling Genson to let Andy sleep. That they had time.

Now, apparently, there wasn't any time.

Again, confusion trickled through him.

The woman stepped in front of Andy and stared directly into his eyes. A chill scuttled under his skin like thousands of tiny black spiders. Something about her seemed just a bit…off. Could just be her gray, smoky gaze, but he wasn't sure.

"Master Sergeant Genson sent the email that you were promoted to the Elite Patrol. Just so happens, we need someone with your skills for a special mission."

"My…skills?"

She nodded and uncrossed her arms only to clasp her hands in front of her. "Yes. Among the Elite, you are the only one with deep diving experience."

Andy opened his mouth and closed it. Not sure how to respond.

The woman sighed and her expression softened. "We want you to join a team to stop the the Gulf Cartel from a leaked cocaine and arms run."

Andy shook his head. "How am I supposed to help with that?"

She shrugged, gestured for the doctor to move away and sat on the rolling stool. "Okay, look. Here's the situation. We need someone who is experienced in deep sea diving in case something goes wrong."

"Wrong with what? I'm not following you. I don't even know who you are."

The woman nodded. "Fair enough, Officer Gains." She stood and clasped her hands in front of her again. "My name is Angela Wexler. President of the Black Water Project." She moved closer, gray eyes fixed on him. "And to answer your other question, a lot could go wrong and we need someone with deep sea knowledge as a precaution. To help the other officers aboard, if needed."

Andy glanced from her to the tall, creepy doctor, and back again. "This isn't an Elite Patrol operation, is it." Not a question.

Angela shrugged, turned toward the only window in the room. "In a lot of ways, it is. A specialized mission near the border. All the officers onboard will be from the Elite. So, yes…I would consider it an Elite Patrol operation." She looked at Andy, smiled. "Except you'll be getting paid for it."

He blinked. "Paid? I'm already getting paid for my job. I don't underst—"

"Up front, and once the mission is complete, Officer Gains. This isn't a salaried position any longer."

Not everything was quite clicking together and he blamed the residue of whatever drug they used to knock him out. Foggy. Sluggish. His mind plodded along in an aimless fashion while he tried to come to grips with, well…whatever the hell was going on.

Apparently, he was a mercenary of sorts now…

"Of course," Angela said and sat back down on the rolling stool, "you can decline this offer. No harm, no foul. You will return to Post 143 and live out the rest of your life catching petty criminals as a lower-class Border Patrol Officer with no chances of advancement."

Andy ran a hand through his short hair. "So, you're saying do this, or live in poverty?"

"What I'm saying, Officer Gains, is if you participate in this mission you will never have to sit in a hot post again. You'll be a hero. A very well-paid hero."

Images of his children galloped through his mind, displacing the receding fog. Of them all playing at the park. Of them catching sunfish at a local farmer's pond. Of Christmases watching their faces light up with every gift. All of which became rare when he accepted the border patrol job.

He leveled his gaze on Angela. "How much?"

Her smoky gray eyes held him in sway. "Enough."

CHAPTER 4

Andy didn't like them.

With all the macho bravado they tossed around, it was like being stuck in the Patrol Academy all over again. They acted like he was trying to secretly cut their throats while they weren't looking so needed to show him they were "tough guys".

Of course, he hadn't gotten to know the guys yet, but first impressions weren't that stellar.

He let them make fools of themselves and went about getting ready for the briefing in a half hour. Which meant taking a piss and running through the shower quick. He smelled…swampy. Even to himself.

They blindfolded him, so Andy had no clue where he was, or even if still in America. Although, the time spent in the van or whatever vehicle they herded him off in wasn't too long. Maybe a couple of hours. However, he couldn't be entirely sure. They might have taken him across the border into Mexico for all he knew.

While the other six guys hooted and laughed, each one apparently trying to be louder than the next, Andy grabbed the gear laid out for him, a towel from the locker room shelves, and took a shower.

He was just pulling up his black cargo pants when a man with slicked back blond hair sauntered over from the six guys bullshitting not far away. Though the look on the man's face fell from amused to serious in a blink. Andy straightened, ready for confrontation.

"You must be the new guy," Mr. Slicked Backed Hair said.

Andy nodded. "I guess." He slipped into a black, Therma Cool, long sleeve shirt. "And you are?"

The blond guy wasn't much taller than Andy and his build less bulky. The man had the body of a lanky gunslinger. His pale blue eyes never left Andy. "Brent Holland. I'm leading this team."

Andy cocked an eyebrow. "Nice to meet you?"

Brent chuckled, though his pale blue eyes revealed a coldness Andy wasn't prepared for. "You're for support only. If you step out of line, I'll shoot you myself. Understand?"

Andy shook his head. "What the hell are you—"

The man was like a striking viper. His hand was around Andy's throat, pinning Andy against the lockers lightning quick. For being so lanky, the guy was strong.

Andy gripped Brent's arm, was about to twist and knee the bastard in the crotch, when the man said, "This mission is the most important mission of your goddamn life. Hear me? 'Cause if you need it beat into you, I'm sure those guys over there will lend a hand."

Never in all his time as a Border Patrol Officer was he threatened, until now. And it came with being part of the Elite Patrol. He wondered what it would take to get out of this mess and forget it all? Leave the Border and just go get a job elsewhere. Could he even request being discharged right now?

After some thought, he doubted it.

Andy glared directly into Brent's eyes. "Get your fucking hands off me."

Brent grunted. "Or what? What are you gonna do, amigo?"

Andy, gaze still holding Brent's, smiled. "This."

He wrenched the hand off his throat and twisted Brent's arm away. The man howled in pain, went to throw a punch, but Andy dodged it. Brent's fist struck the locker with a meaty thunk. Andy sent a couple of hard jabs into Brent's stomach and side, kneed the bastard away far enough to round house kick the guy in the face.

Brent dropped to the floor, holding his face. He spat blood onto the white tiles.

"Holy shit," someone said in an Irish accent. "Did he just round house Brent?"

A few seconds ticked by with only Brent grunting in pain, then they came at Andy. A couple of them much larger, the rest about Brent's size. Didn't matter, though. It was five against one.

"Motherfucker," one of the larger men growled, storming directly at Andy. A long, pink scar twisted diagonally across his brutish face. "I'm gonna—"

"You're not gonna do shit," Brent said and stood.

The men stopped and turned to the man.

Brent rubbed his lower jaw, wiped away a runner of blood and snorted. "Hell of a kick. Where'd you learn to do that?"

Andy, muscles still tense, lowered his fists a bit. "Studied Muay Thai since I was twelve." Well, he hadn't studied the art for a couple of years now, but at least his body hadn't gone too lax on him. Sometimes it was all about muscle memory. That didn't stop the ache burning in his left leg from overstretching.

"Well," Brent said, "it shows." He turned his attention to the other five. "Shake this man's hand. He's part of the team, so treat him like it."

"But you—" the big guy with the scar across his face began.

"You know I test anyone new to the team, Willie," Brent said. "Andy, here, just passed the test." Brent gave Andy a nod.

Andy nodded back, though still confused. Attacking someone was considered a test? Genson did so back at the post, but that felt different than Brent's attack or test. Whatever the fuck it was. Brent seemed angry and hateful while Genson's appeared functionary and hesitant.

Why they felt the need to attack him to test him, he'd never know.

Bastards.

The big guy, Willie, sighed and extended a massive hand. His fingers were like bratwursts. Andy shook it, his hand disappearing into that giant paw. The man's grip was firm, but to Andy's surprise, not crushing. Willie gave a nod, stepped away, and the next guy towered over him. Just about as big as Willie.

"Ben," the man said in a deep rumble of a voice and extended his equally massive hand.

Andy shook it, nodded and the next guy stepped forward. This one was about the same height as Andy, though skinnier, wore glasses, and had a shock of blue dyed hair.

"I'm Sully," the man said with a faint Irish accent. They shook hands. Sully moved on.

A guy with jet black hair in a messy spike patted Andy's shoulder. "Name's Eldon, man."

Eldon stepped away to reveal a man just a hair shorter than Andy. Huskier too. With his long gray hair and beard, he could have either been an obscure wizard or old warrior in some grimdark fantasy novel or another. His bloodshot green eyes surveyed Andy for a moment.

"Les," he said. He did not extend his hand. Instead, the man turned and walked away.

It was just odd. How they immediately just did as Brent said without even a qualm. Well, except for old Les, of course. That guy, Andy might have to keep an eye on.

They left him to get dressed and he eventually followed them to a large room with a round table. Reminded him too much of King Arthur and the Knight of the Round Table thing. Brent moved around so that he sat right next to Andy. Which was weird, but Andy tried not to let it get to him too much. He didn't know these people and observance, rather than reaction, was what mattered more. Until he figured them out, he'd be only speculating.

Once everyone was seated, Angela Wexler bustled into the room. The door swung closed behind her. Everyone watched her stride to the front of the room in front of a large white screen.

"Time is shorter than initially expected," she said and gestured at Andy. "As you know, we have a new addition to the team. Andy Gains.

He's our deep-sea diving expert. If anything goes wrong and you're forced to abandon ship…listen to him. Understood?"

The guys nodded, though none spoke up.

Ms. Wexler nodded back and said, "Good. He's part of the team now, so I expect you all to treat him as such. Now, to the mission…"

She stepped aside, the lights dimmed, and an image of a Hispanic man appeared on the screen. Black hair slicked back and a cigarette near his grinning mouth. His dark eyes were as blank and predatory as a great white shark.

"As most of you know, except for maybe Andy, this is Carlito Guerra, Lord of The Cartel Del Golfo, or the Gulf Cartel, in English," Wexler said. "As I'm sure you all know, this Cartel is one of the largest and fastest drug and arms runners in history. And that's just on land…"

"Now it's underwater," Brent whispered. Barely audible.

Andy frowned, though didn't look at the man. How would Brent know before Wexler telling him so? Strange.

Andy pretended like he didn't hear while Wexler continued. "Again, most of you know about the Black Water Project. Though, for Andy's sake, I'll fill you in a little on what we do." Still standing next to the screen, the image switched from Carlito Guerra to an up-close look at an angler fish. Its translucent teeth open, opaque eyes seemingly glaring directly at the camera. A menacing looming creature if ever there was one.

"In 2022, we founded the Black Water Project to build the best and safest submersible transportation in the world. We achieved that goal in 2023 when our first submersible, the Echo Sub 1, broke the forty thousand feet barrier no one managed to get by in the Challenger Deep. It did so with ease. The team spent two weeks in the deepest black waters and collected many new specimens of fish as well as sand and rock from the Mariana Trench itself." The image of the angler fish faded and a new one appeared. This one of something Andy had never seen before. A white, scrawny fish, though it appeared to have squid-like tentacles all along its belly.

"This guy," Wexler said, "put us on the map as one of the leading oceanic research facilities in the world. The cure for ALS? It was extracted from the blood of this anomaly. We later dubbed the species Lou, after Lou Gehrig, of course."

"C'mon," Brent whispered, again, barely audible, beside Andy. "C'mon."

Andy's frown deepened. What was wrong with the guy? Maybe he was bored because he knew Black Water's history? Or maybe…it was something else. The tension gathering in the room signaled to Andy it might be something more than just the rehash of the company's history getting under Brent's skin. The guy was antsy. As though time was of the essence and he needed to be somewhere else right now.

"Lou helped fund our greatest feat of forty-five thousand feet, where we stumbled across this…" The image changed from Lou to a fluorescent pink worm-like creature. "The videos of her are amazing. She can change colors. Pink, according to our scientists, means she's content. Blue meant she was angry or scared. Regardless, she helped to eliminate most forms of cancer. Thankfully, we were able to duplicate the cell structures and clone her for further research instead of harvesting her species. We called her Cinder because her extracts literally burn away the cancer cells. From her, we rose to the number one top research facility in the world."

She surveyed the group and the image on the screen switched again, this time revealing the mouth of what appeared to be a ragged, rocky hole underwater.

"This is Worm Hole Six," Wexler said. "There are, so far as we are aware at this time, eight more of these holes near the Mexico coastal cities of Matamoros and Tampico. Recently discovered by drones and dinged as ocean floor anomalies. The US Government has reasons to believe these holes might actually be tunnels for Carlito's drug runners." She paused, as if the guys would ooo and ahhh over the revelation. When no one said anything, she continued, "That's where we come in. You'll be using our Echo Sub 10 to infiltrate the tunnels and find out where they lead."

Andy thought about it a second or two and said, "Could they have already been there and no one noticed until now?"

Brent issued a quiet sigh, but Wexler smiled. An almost genuine smile. Probably as close as anyone would ever see, Andy figured. "Yes. That's very possible. Sink holes in the ocean happen just like on land. But we were hired to investigate, so that's what we're going to do, Officer Gains."

If she wasn't paying him a million dollars to follow orders, he would have walked long ago.

A million dollars. The money would help with, well, everything. The piles of bills, his kids' schooling and food, and…he could give them a better life than strictly working for the Border Patrol. He could…

You're a mercenary now, a thin voice whispered in his head. He tried to shut it out, but it barreled through his mental block. *You're a mercenary. Dishonorable and a cheat. What you're doing is illegal.*

All true and he despised the word mercenary. But it was true, and he'd have to live with that. For his family…he'd live with it. Sometimes survival meant venturing outside the box of the norm and staking your claim. In Andy's case, it all just kind of fell into his lap. Whether he liked it or not, he was a mercenary.

Maybe a mercenary could do good things, though? He liked to think so.

Case in point with the tunnels. If they were made by the Cartel, then he was doing a good thing by trying to figure out how and why. And, if there really was an illegal operation going on, it would make his decision even more valid.

"Elite Officer Sullivan," Wexler said.

The guy with the blue hair—Sully?— nodded. "Aye, love."

"You'll need to meet with our engineers to learn the operations of Echo Sub 10 before you deploy."

Sully snapped a salute. "Fuckin' A."

Wexler blinked, though, Andy noted, her expression deepened a bit. She lingered on Sully longer than necessary. Staring at each other. Transfixed.

Uh-oh, Andy thought, bemused.

Finally, Brent stood and said, "Right. Well, let's get this show on the road, eh, amigos?"

The man was as white as could be, and yet had an odd, very subtle Spanish accent going on. A small detail which gave Andy pause for a minute or two. Then everything happened really fast.

Wexler dismissed the meeting and led them to a massive cavern-like area with a deep pool at the center. A submersible unit sat near the right edge of the round pool. A few people stood waiting near the submersible. Men and women. All of them with about the same stoic expression plastered on their face.

"This will just be a quick training course," Wexler said as she strode ahead. "Get you all familiar with the controls and confines of Echo Sub 10." She stopped in front of the submersible and turned to face the men. "It's our largest, fastest sub. In any case, I leave you in the hands of the real experts. You will deploy in approximately two hours. We will keep radio contact throughout the mission." She smiled. "Godspeed." And, with that, she bustled away, moderate heels clicking on the concrete and echoing throughout the cavernous space.

The men faced the small group of people and everyone just kind of stared at each other until Brent cleared his throat and stepped forward. "Probably should get this show on the road, eh, amigos?"

It was like a quarterback just shouted hut-hut. Everyone shot forward and dispersed.

Andy stood and watched Eldon and Sully and a large black man discuss the mechanics of Echo Sub 10. He even caught a bit of the conversation.

"Echolocation, aye?" Sully planted his hands on his narrow hips. "Like dolphins?"

The black man smiled. "Exactly that. Through a few trials in murky water, I noticed the sub would bump into objects before the pilot saw anything. So, I used what I learned about dolphins while working for a rehabilitation center in Orlando. That, and studying bats in college helped. The other subs have Echo in the name, but this is the only one that actually lives up to the name."

Sully whistled. "Fuckin' brilliant, man. Absolutely." He snorted and gave the man a nudge. "Tis like the Bat Sub, aye?"

The black man chuckled and shook his head. "If you say so. Here, let me show you the controls."

The two men entered Echo Sub 10.

Eldon ran a hand through his thick, black hair and followed. The man was, after all, the sub expert and would be the pilot. A bit of irritation was visible on Eldon's gaunt face. Though Andy could tell, it wasn't his first rodeo dealing with Sully.

Brent and the others were chatting with the other people. There was laughter and jokes aplenty. Nothing in the way of teaching and learning, which Andy thought was supposed to be going on. He ventured closer to the group, overhearing a conversation or two.

A short, thin man told Brent, "Should all be in order."

Brent chuckled. "Well, it fucking better be, Clark. Or it's your ass."

Andy frowned, finding that little exchange odd, but didn't stop to listen more. He wanted to cruise around them and take in what was going on. Because he felt like the mission was a cover for something else. Brent's actions and small quips got Andy's mind reeling a bit. Curiosity took hold with hooked claws.

He'd come back around to Brent soon enough.

Still, he hoped he was wrong and they were all discussing last night's baseball game, or something. Another thing he noted…most of them appeared to know each other. And quite well.

Andy sauntered by Willie, the big guy with the scar across his face, yucking it up with a woman less than half his size.

"When this is all over," Willie said, "I'll take ya on that date ya want to go on." He hur-hurred and added, "Just messin' round, Rach. But seriously, ya wanna bone?"

Rach (short for Rachel?) did not appear amused in the slightest. She crossed her arms over her chest and distanced herself from the big man a bit. "I…I don't do that kind of thing. A date sounds nice."

To that, the piggish brute reared in a bout of howling laughter.

It wasn't funny. Not to the girl. Not to Andy.

He moved on.

Les, the husky older man with all that gray hair and beard, clapped a young guy on the back and said, "Got any more of that whisky, brother?"

The young man, maybe in his late twenties, smiled, adjusted his glasses and said, "Two bottles. Same price."

"Well," Les said in a hearty tone that made Andy envision a Viking warrior. "Be sure to pack 'em in the sub, boy. This is gonna be a long one."

"Five hundred," the young man said. "I'll even throw in a glass."

"Ya think I'm gonna share? No glass. Here, boy." Les shoved a bunch of bills at the young man. "Pack 'em in the back. That's where I'll be."

Andy, despite himself, smiled and moved on to Ben.

The other big man of the group, though much more reserved than Willie. He talked quietly with another man, though too low for Andy to hear in mere passing. He didn't want to linger too much so returned to Brent.

"Everything is in place," Clark said and his gaze darted to Andy. He froze, eyes widening.

Brent straightened and turned. He noticed Andy and grunted. When the man turned back to Clark, he said, "The kid is with us. Don't worry."

After some time, the group of men gathered into Echo Sub 10 and a crane lifted and placed them in the deep pool. Andy had no idea how deep it was but guessed at least a thousand feet. At any rate, he couldn't see the bottom.

Then they sank like a rock.

The small sub wasn't as compact as Andy initially thought. Instead, it was rather roomy in the passenger area. The read held all the supplies. Water. Food. Ammo. Not to mention seven deep dive suits. Suits a bit more advanced than Andy had ever used. More like thin layered mechs. But that was ridiculous. No one had really come up with that kind of tech yet.

Or had they?

Andy never really paid too much attention to technical advancements. Just what was spouted on the news from time to time. When he was at Post 143, they had, maybe, a half hour of leisure time. And that was if you wanted to risk losing that half hour of sleep. Something Andy didn't do often, though felt he needed to be at least somewhat competent in world events. Though, the more he watched the more he wished he didn't know.

The world got itself into a mess years ago and things were just getting worse. Sooner or later, Andy figured, too many red buttons would be pressed at once and...well...

Ah, but he tried not to think too much about that. There was nothing he could do anyway.

Buzzing ripped him from his thoughts.

"Eight hundred feet," Sully said. "Pressure stabilization still hasn't—
"

"Hold on," Eldon muttered, as he tapped something on the digital panel and pulled back on the crescent wheel.

The entire sub tilted, though despite Eldon's dramatic pull on the horseshoe wheel, the shift was barely noticeable. The only inkling at the severity of the tilt could be found looking through the bridge's curved windshield. Nothing dramatic, though a spec of light which meant the surface. It meant Echo Sub 10 was aimed in the right direction, but...

Red lights flickered throughout the sub. A thin bray sounded.

And it was getting harder to breathe.

"The fuck you two idiots doing up there?" Brent called. He shifted in his seat, chest rising and falling a bit more than usual.

Indeed, everyone's chests fell and expanded more and more while they tried to adjust to the changing pressure and increasing lack of oxygen.

Andy's ears crackled with the pressure changes.

"They dropped us too soon," Eldon said. "We didn't get the boosters running beforehand, so we sank." He tapped something on the digital panel. "So, we didn't get the pressure stabilization going in time. Sorry about the steep ascension, but we need to get to a viable depth before working stabilizing."

A tick of silence.

Then Willie spouted, "What?"

Brent sighed, pinched the bridge of his nose with a thumb and forefinger. "I swear, your brain is the size of a peanut, Willie."

The large man's barrel chest heaved. "What...what's that supposed to mean?" He blinked. "Why can't I breathe good?"

Again, Brent sighed. He shot Andy a bemused look and shook his head. Andy smiled in return. As suspected, the oaf was a bit slow. Nothing drastic, but slow enough to be irritating. How Willie passed the exams in the Patrol Academy was beyond Andy.

Eventually, the pressure lessened, and Sully was able to stabilize everything. Everyone breathed like normal again.

Near the rear of the sub, inches from the specialized diving suits, Les took a quick swig from a brown bottle, capped it and tucked it under his seat with the efficiency of a true alcoholic. Andy shook his head, adjusted himself a bit and found Brent staring directly at him.

There came a short, but very awkward space of silence.

"Your file says you're from Minnesota."

Andy shrugged. "Yeah. We moved to Texas when I got the Border Patrol job."

Brent nodded, deep blue eyes never straying from Andy. "Then how are you so experienced in deep sea diving?"

He knew the subject would pop up sooner or later, but he didn't expect it from Brent. Test or no test, the guy didn't appear to know anything about Andy in the locker room. Unless, of course, Brent was playing a part to appeal to the other five. Which made sense, in a way. He needed the main team to accept him in order to lead them effectively. Something like that, perhaps.

Cool air whooshed through the small sub and Andy said, "Started in the lakes up there. Deepest I ever got was five hundred feet. During college, I signed on for deep sea classes in the South Pacific." Again, he shrugged. "I just happened to be good at it."

Brent cocked an eyebrow. "So why didn't you pursue a career in diving instead of Border Patrol?"

"What does it matter?" Andy's fists slowly clenched and unclenched. He didn't know what Brent's intentions were, but the guy might as well have had a large, hot light aimed at Andy's face while grilling him with all the questions.

Brent leaned back in his seat as the air gradually eased in breathability. "Well, if I'm to trust you with my life, don't I have the right to know some things?"

He was considering telling Brent the reasons for abandoning deep sea diving for the Border Patrol when Sully said, "Fuckin' hell. They just dropped us in. Like sink or swim, ya bastards."

"We're stabilizing," Eldon said. "Another ten seconds and we should be free to dive."

Andy sighed. "I chose the Border Patrol because I got married and had kids. Diving didn't pay the bills."

Brent leaned forward, grinning. "Take it you agreed to this because you wanted a better life for your kids, yes?"

"I can't disagree with that," Andy said. "Everything I do is for them."

Brent gave a firm nod. "Of course you do." He crossed his arms over his chest and leaned back again. "You're a good dad. Want to make sure your kids are well fed and have a nice roof over their heads."

"That's right."

"I'll drink to that," Les muttered and slammed back a shot or two of whiskey. He hid the bottle, as though no one noticed. Everyone noticed. Even Brent. Though nobody said anything.

Yes, Andy realized, they were all a team before he entered the picture. No matter how they tried to appear different, they've worked together before. They were aware of each other's quirks. That much was apparent just by the subtle glance from Brent to Les. Perhaps their time as a team was brief, but enough to remember things like Les's slight drinking problem.

"So, Good Dad," Brent said, arms still crossed. "What would your kids think knowing their dad wasn't as honorable and good as they think he is?"

Andy's heart stuttered. "What the hell is that supposed to mean?"

Grinning, Brent shrugged. "Guess we'll see, eh, amigo?"

A frown sunk into Andy's face. His stomach churned. "See what, exactly?"

The grin faded from Brent's face. "We'll see how well you listen from this point forward." He uncrossed his arms and leaned forward. "Don't worry, they're fine. For now."

Rage boiled through Andy. He shot forward, hand gripping Brent's throat. He slammed the man against the metal wall.

"Ah, hell," Les muttered and scooted closer.

Brent threw a punch into Andy's side hard enough to send him stumbling.

Willie whooped and shoved Andy back toward Brent.

But it was Les who caught him and placed him in his seat.

"Enough," the older man rumbled, facing Brent. "That is some horrid shit you just told the boy. We're not the goddamn mob."

Brent winked at Les. "Maybe we're the only mob left."

"Prepare to dive," Sully shouted.

Les growled and plopped down in his seat. He buckled the three-point harness.

Andy, side aching, followed suit. So did Brent, all the while glowering at Andy. Andy's gaze lowered. He couldn't look at the bastard right now.

If what Brent said was true and his kids might be in danger if he didn't listen…the thought alone chilled the very marrow of his bones. *If* it was true. For all Andy knew, the man was messing with him. Playing up the bully angle to make sure Andy fell in line with what Brent felt was required. Whatever that was.

Les was right. Brent might as well have been a mob boss giving some subordinate a warning. Brent even welcomed it.

So, what now?

If he requested to leave, would they let him? Somehow, he doubted it. He was stuck now. Money trapped him. Always, it was money. But it was money he wanted for his children. Brent hit the nail on the head there. He was a good dad, and all he wanted was for his kids to have a decent life and not go hungry. Like any parent worth their salt, all he wanted was to raise his children in the best way possible.

The Echo Sub 10 shot downward like a bullet until an alarm blared.

"Bottom is twenty meters," Sully said. "Pull up, ya fecker!"

Eldon muttered something and tapped the panel. Nothing happened. He muttered again.

There was no doubt in Andy's mind they were about to crash into the bottom of the pool. He braced himself for impact, gripping the straps of the harness. In the back of his mind he thought about the dive suits and how he'd get them on the crew before they were crushed to death by the water pressure or during a panic if they were taking on water.

"Fucking *work*." Eldon punched the panel. "You souped up piece of sh—"

From what Andy could see, the panel flickered red, then purple. A short beep came from a ceiling speaker.

And through the windshield...the bottom of the pool grew larger and larger.

"Oh, just fuckin' lovely," Sully shouted. "Ya broke the damned thing."

Eldon didn't respond to the Irishman, instead he began counting backward from five.

"Five."

The entire sub shuddered.

"Four."

"The feck ya countin' for, boyo?" Sully said.

"Three."

The bottom of the pool filled the windshield.

"Two."

Andy sucked in a deep breath.

"One."

Eldon simultaneously pulled the crescent wheel back and tapped a blinking blue light on the panel Andy hadn't noticed before. The Echo Sub 10 slammed to a halt and leveled out, jarring Andy from the inside out. The stop was so abrupt, everyone vomited. The stench was enough to get Andy spewing a second time. He wiped his chin with a trembling hand and sat there for the longest time. He didn't look at anyone, nor did they ask how each other was doing. He imagined everyone was in a mild state of shock. Even Eldon.

Through the speakers, Angela Wexler said, "What the hell happened? Eldon? Sully? You copy?"

Sully groaned, sat up in his seat a bit and tapped a green phone icon on his side of the panel. "Aye. 'Bout fuckin' died is all."

"All our alarms went off at once up here," Wexler said. "Eldon?"

Eldon managed to sit up, though just barely. "The unit sank upon release. I didn't have enough time to set the boosters and stabilize pressure before our descent. We were six meters from hitting bottom, but I got the boosters working in time."

"You didn't set it to gradual boost?"

Eldon sighed. "Didn't have time. The panel blanked out on me. Had to use a different route access."

Sully snorted. "He punched it."

"I did not," Eldon said and snapped a glare at Sully.

Sully chuckled, and shrugged.

Through the speakers, a man said, "Your panel went out because of the pressure issue. Please be sure to stabilize before descending."

Sully face-palmed and flipped the nearest speaker off. Andy couldn't help but smile. "Would've done it too it someone hadn't dropped our arses without warning."

Wexler came back on. "There will be no warnings out in the field, gentlemen. I issued the abrupt drop. Though, I expected both pilot and co-pilot to be paying attention."

"Listen here, you starry cu—"

Eldon slapped a hand over Sully's mouth. "We'll be better prepared next time. Thanks. Ready for the exercises now."

A pause, then Wexler said, "Initiating sequences now. Please complete each task with utmost efficiency."

"Aye," Sully said and tapped the red phone icon. The speakers clicked.

Everyone sat in silence for a few seconds.

Andy breathed in the stench of puke and tried not to upchuck again. His throat worked against his rising gorge.

"Okay," Eldon said. "Looks like that's our first marker."

A red light blinked in front of them.

"Let's hurry it up," Brent said, looking just as green as Andy felt.

The training didn't take long.

CHAPTER 5

Tampico, Mexico, wasn't what Andy expected.

Not the dusty old Mexican town they portrayed in the movies. On the contrary, it was beautiful. The palm trees and architecture alone captivated him. And, despite it being so hot, he could almost see himself living there. Retirement, perhaps?

That was a laugh. The way things were going, he'd never be able to retire. Not with the cost of living and food, and medicines. No, the system would work him until it chewed him up and spat out his dusty bones. Shitty, but that was life.

Regardless, Andy imagined himself in a hammock between two palm trees, gently swaying in a warm, humid breeze flowing off the Gulf. Maybe he had a cold drink in his hand. Maybe a book. Or, perhaps, he was snoozing away the afternoon.

And it was in Tampico when everything changed.

The team sat in a small, sweaty cantina called La Guarida. The Lair. A place which did suit the stereotypical Mexican bar. Less than eight customers, all chatting quietly with the bartender. A single ceiling fan creaked and groaned overhead. Everything appeared to be coated in a thin layer of dust. The smell of beer underlined the sour reek of sweat and body odor.

Everyone except Brent nursed a lukewarm beer. He filled a shot glass with tequila and knocked it back. After his second shot, he turned the shot glass around and around with his fingers. It whispered on the wooden table. He was about to pour his third shot when Sully placed a hand on the man's arm.

"I like me a few shots too, but yer on the job, man."

Brent's weary eyes lifted, gaze fixing on Sully. "Get your hand off me, you fucking mick."

Sully blinked, pulled his hand away, glanced at Andy, and then to Eldon. "The hell?"

Eldon frowned, attention on Brent. "What is it?"

Brent shook his head and knocked back another shot.

One beer ahead of everyone else, Les nudged Brent. "Better get to talkin', boy. You said you had more intel about the mission, remember?"

Brent huffed out a weak chuckle. "Yeah, I did, didn't I." He tilted the tequila bottle to pour another shot, but Les took it from him before a drop was spilled.

With movements so quick, Andy barely noticed them, Brent turned and punched the older man in the face twice before Les shoved the guy off his chair. Brent crashed to the dusty floor. Les shook his head and slammed the bottle onto the table.

"I might like my booze, but at least I can handle it."

Brent shot to his feet and shoved a gun to Les's temple. "Who said I couldn't handle it, asshole?"

Les winked at Andy. "I did, boy." He grunted, took a swig of warm beer and added, "If you're gonna shoot me, hurry the hell up. I ain't got all day. S'posed to be shoving off here in less than an hour."

Brent, face getting redder and redder, lowered the gun, holstered it and plopped back down on his chair.

None of the patrons appeared to notice.

Maybe that was why Brent picked the place. No one there cared, nor wanted to. They just talked amongst themselves like the rest of the world didn't exist. How many foul plots had passed through the little cantina without them knowing? Or, maybe they knew and just didn't care.

Despite the three quick shots of tequila, Brent didn't appear to be buzzing or drunk. His focus on each person was sharp as a razor. His blue eyes demanded attention.

"This isn't a mission to locate tunnels and find where they lead." His gaze drifted over the team, lingering a bit on Andy before moving on. "We're gonna help the Cartel."

All the air slowly leaked out of Andy's lungs.

The entire table tripped over the edge into silence. No one looked at each other. Brent sighed and leaned back. His chair gave a tired squawk. The rest of the cantina went on about its business. The regulars never missed a beat in their conversations. Glasses clinked while a sleepy-eyed bartender dipped them in water and wiped them off with a stained white towel. He flung the towel over a narrow shoulder, filled both glasses with beer and scooted them in front of a couple of men in dusty blue jumpsuits.

Overhead, the fan creaked.

Sully gave a soft whistle, chugged the rest of his beer and slammed the glass down. "Fuck it. I'm in."

"Whoa," Les said and patted Sully's shoulder. "Hold on, now. This ain't a mission now. It's workin' for drug lords." His bushy gray eyebrows knitted together, iron gaze fixed on Brent. "Don't know about any of the rest of ya, but I'm not a piece of shit."

Brent crossed his arms over his chest, and smiled. Either he was finally catching that buzz, or his worries were all an act. Andy voted for the latter.

"You each get six million dollars. Half deposited into a bank account of your choice as soon as you give me the okay. The rest will be deposited when the job is done."

Les opened his mouth and closed it. A long breath blew from his flaring nostrils. He glared at his beer, knocked it down, took the bottle of tequila from Brent and took a hearty swig. The older man slammed the bottle down and blew out a breath. Les pointed a thick finger at Brent.

"I only worked with you on one mission, boy. How do I know I can trust ya?"

Brent's cheeks puffed out in a heavy breath. He snagged the bottle of tequila back and drank. Done, he pointed right back at Les.

"You can't." Brent placed the bottle down. Didn't slam it. His focus was still razor sharp. "But who can ever trust anyone in this world, right? Look, I didn't let you down in Iran, now did I?"

Les huffed out a breath, opened his mouth, but—

"And," Brent said, "before you say that was different, I'd like to point out that the Government are the worst criminals. Not just our Government either. All those bastards would rather slit their own mother's throats than lose face or, God forbid, any money."

Andy frowned and looked at Les. The old man shook his head. He stole the bottle of tequila back and drank. This time upending it for several long pulls. The bottle was almost half empty by the time he slammed it down and expelled a long breath.

"Need proof, boy," Les said.

"Proof," Brent said and chuckled. "I forget all you ol' timers want proof. Well, here…" He brought out his phone, tapped it a bit and slid it across the table to Les.

The older man leaned forward, squinting.

Andy thought about lifting it up for him, then decided not to. The guy would probably take offence to such a gesture. No matter how kind. Sometimes men of his age were fickle bastards. Those refusing to face the facts they were getting too old for certain things. Like reading. Maybe they needed glasses, like Les, but, somehow, it would be too unmanly to accept the fact. Andy's stepdad was the exact same way. Old workhorse, sure. But there came a time when that horse needed to ease up and accept that if it pressed too hard, it'd break a leg and wind up lame.

And when a horse wound up lame…

Les guzzled down a few more swigs of tequila and handed Brent his phone back. "Fine."

The other two, Willie and Ben, nodded almost sagely. Willie, being a half-wit and all, probably didn't even know where he was. Bunched in front of him were a dozen beer glasses. Which made Andy wonder how the man's stomach was feeling with all that Mexican beer sloshing around in it? He knew from experience not to drink another country's water or drinks unless bottled. Bad things happened. Like—

As if on cue, Willie let go a loud belch. His eyes rolled in their meaty sockets. His hands fell to his stomach. Sweat beaded his sloping forehead. A squealing groan came from his stomach.

Everyone turned their attention to the big man, even, Andy noted, the chatty regulars.

"Ya alright, ya big bastard?" Sully asked and scooted his chair away from the table a bit.

Willie swayed. Another groan rumbled out of his stomach. "I...I..." The big man shot out of his chair, and stumbled around. "I gotta *shit!*"

"Restoom está atrás," the bartender said, his sleepy gaze shifting away from Willie as he pointed down a narrow hall.

Andy wasn't sure if the giant man could even squeeze through it.

A small fart squeaked out. Willie clapped his hands to his butt. "What the fuck is he *saying*?"

"Restroom is in the back," Brent said, as he stood and led Willie to the narrow hallway.

To Andy's surprise, the guy shimmied down the hall without getting stuck.

Once Brent made sure Willie was in the bathroom, he returned to the table and plopped down in his chair.

"So, what's the verdict?"

Eldon lowered his head and didn't say anything.

"You know my vote," Sully said and lit a cigarette.

Les shook his head. "Guess ya know mine too."

"Sure," Ben, the second largest dude, said out of nowhere. There wasn't anything in front of him except a half empty water bottle. His brown eyes drifted from person to person, face expressionless.

Brent's focus sharpened on Andy. "What about you, new guy? Ready to get the windfall of a lifetime and secure a future for your kids?"

"Wait," Sully blurted. "He's got kiddies?" The Irishman turned to Andy. "The fuck ya joinin' up with us for, ya arse? Go back to them kiddies and forget this shit."

Brent's gaze burrowed into Andy like a carnivorous worm. And, although Sully's recommendation to quit and take care of the kids was tempting, Andy eventually said, "Is everything confidential?"

Brent grinned. "Of course." Might as well be the Devil's grin.

Andy frowned. This was worse than being a pseudo mercenary. This was going full bore, head-first into a pool filled with ravenous bull sharks. If he accepted, he'd be a criminal. His life in the Elite Patrol cut short. Unless, of course, it was all bullshit. Which, as he sat there in the hot cantina with its mingling stenches of beer, sweat, and piss, Andy doubted everything. Especially his random promotion.

Even if it was Genson who originally announced it.

And now, he was trapped with this group of men about to help the Gulf Cartel run drugs or guns, or whatever.

By the gleam in Brent's eyes, Andy figured if he got up and walked out, a bullet would find the back of his head the second he stepped through the door. The man was practically daring him to do it too. The devilish grin lengthened a tad.

Finally, Andy looked away and said, "Fine."

Brent let out a woot and clapped his hands. "Alright, boys! Next round is on me. Whatcha drinkin'?"

Les stood. "Think I'm gonna get some air." The older man left the cantina without another word.

Andy stood, about to follow Les out, but Brent shot a hand out, viper quick, and grabbed his arm. Brent's fingertips dug into Andy's forearm to the point of hurting. Andy's free hand fell to the butt of his sidearm.

"Let go," Andy said, trying to keep his tone even and failing miserably.

Brent, noticing where Andy's free hand rested, snorted. "You're going to shoot your employer?" He released Andy's arm and leaned back in his chair. "I think you should stay and get to know everyone better. After all…you're part of the team now, right?"

Andy glanced at Ben. No help there. His gaze fell on Eldon. All he got was a shrug from the guy.

"Oh, sit your arse down, boyo," Sully spouted and stood. He rubbed Andy's shoulders. "Shit, though, ain't a tense one? Like a goddamn loaded spring."

Andy shrugged away from Sully and sat down. Directly in front of him, Brent smiled.

"What's your poison, amigo?"

CHAPTER 6

Almost a half-bottle of rum later, Andy learned that Ben was also from Iowa. A farm boy. That didn't surprise him much. What threw him off guard, though, was Ben had a PHD in mechanical engineering. He might be the second largest on the team, but he appeared to be the smartest. He joined the Elite Patrol because he was also good with guns and knives, though he preferred fists over deadly weapons. Andy liked him.

Sully's story was a bit…different. Born in Ireland, the guy grew up with loving parents and a strong work ethic. "Poor as fuck," Sully said. "But ya know it's not much fretted over on my island."

"You mean Ireland," Brent said and sipped at a piss warm beer. Judging by his grimace, Andy was happy he chose the rum.

"Yup," Sully said. "It's mine." It's *mione*.

Andy opened his mouth to tell them those lines were from a movie when Sully flapped a hand. He slammed back a shot of whiskey and winked at Andy. "That's from a movie, ya know."

Andy chuckled and was about to ask Brent's story, when Sully continued, "By the time I was sixteen, I be runnin' wit the Greys."

"Greys?" Andy asked, unable to help himself.

Sully huffed out a breath and squinted at the empty chair in front of him. Where Willie was supposed to be. "Old gang, really. But good lads, ya know? We stole, aye, but we gave poorer people what we took."

"Like Robin Hood," Andy said, intrigued.

Sully snapped his fingers. "Aye! Like that ol' English dolt, indeed. Anyway, I got bored with all that and hitched a boat ride over to America. Got a degree in Marine Biology and did some honest research work for a couple of years. I just kinda applied for an Elite Patrol position after that and got accepted. Not sure how. I shot everything they told me to, so maybe it was that. Weird, aye?"

Andy nodded. "Yeah."

Brent laughed. "You're a goddamn liar, Sully. You tried more than once to get into the Elite."

Sully knocked back another shot and shook his head. "Shut y'mouth, fecker. I—"

It crashed through the door, wood splinters flying in every direction. The regulars shouted and scattered behind the bar with the tender. Wooden stools rolled every which way.

Andy, Ben, Sully and Brent drew their sidearms, overturned the table and gaped at the creature growling just inside the doorway.

It wasn't a coyter. Much larger and apish in appearance. To Andy, it reminded him of Bigfoot, only not quite as tall. It hunched over like a gorilla, but its head resembled a mountain lion. Though broader and much larger. No doubt a mutation from some experiment or another. Like the coyters. Splicing of different animals in hopes to preserve not one DNA but several. Unfortunately, during such experiments, things go wrong. Sometimes things escape. Sometimes they breed...

Andy had no idea what the creature was growling in the doorway of the cantina. Neither did the others apparently. They all shouted at it, though didn't spout a name of the species. Or nickname.

Andy aimed his pistol at the creature's cat-like head.

A loud roar filled the cantina.

The bartender merely stood there and blinked at it with those sleepy eyes.

Andy had the thing in his sights. His finger crept over the trigger. Genson would be yelling at him to shoot the damn thing. He was taking too long.

"Yeesh," Willie said, shuffling out of the hallway. "Might wanna get some air fresheners in there, man. Don't know what you put in that beer, but—" The big man frowned and turned toward the creature. "What the fuck is that?"

"Fire," Brent shouted.

Without pause, Willie took a knee, drew his pistol and fired off four shots before the creature pounced and slammed into him.

Heart thundering, Andy side-stepped and fired three bullets into its feline skull. Still, it tore into the big man. Willie howled and beat at the beast with his pistol and fist. Blood flew through the air and splattered the bar.

Brent knelt beside Andy and fired twice. Both shots also struck the creature in the head. Ben stormed in, holding up a hand for everyone to cease fire. The man was like a moving mountain to Andy. Kilimanjaro to Willie's Everest. Something like that. Even so, Ben grabbed the beast by the scuff behind its blood smeared head and ripped it off Willie. He tossed it aside like it was nothing but a bag of trash.

Willie rolled away, leaving a blood trail in his wake.

The creature struck the wall by the door, yelped and tried to stand. Blood spewed from its tooth filled mouth and drizzled to the floor. Its green eyes followed Ben as the man moved. He drew his pistol.

The thing tried to stand, tried to fight. In the end, however, it collapsed onto the floor. Blood pooled around it. Its nostrils flared, drawing and expelling ragged breath after ragged breath.

Ben shook his head and hunkered down in front of the beast.

"Uh, Benny-Boy," Sully called. "I don't think it wants to be friends."

Andy watched Ben closely, pistol ready just in case. But, the longer he watched, the less he believed he needed the gun anymore.

Ben holstered his sidearm and gently stroked the top of the creature's head. Andy stood, not believing what he was seeing.

"Acushla," Sully murmured.

"What?" Brent shot a frown at the Irishman.

Sully nodded at Ben and the beast. "Means pulse of m'heart." He sighed. "Look at that."

The creature purred. A deep rumbling, though not as deep as a growl.

"It didn't choose to be what it is," Ben said. His baritone voice ebbed through the foul air. "Look at its sides. It's starving."

Andy stepped to the side and gasped. He hadn't noticed it before during all the commotion, but its ribs poked out from its sleek, black fur. His heart sank a bit, watching the animal's—because that's what it was. An animal. Even if it was many spliced together—labored breathing. The rise and shuddering fall of those ribs filled Andy with a sorrow he hadn't known existed. Ben was right. The animal didn't choose to be what it was. Just like the extinct Siberian tiger didn't choose to be a tiger. It just simply *was*.

Everyone holstered their guns and watched in silence while Ben petted the dying animal until its scant ribs expanded no more.

Ben lowered his head.

Silence, save for the creaking of the ceiling fan, held the old stinky cantina sway for a few seconds.

"I think I'm dyin'," Willie said. He sat with his back against the wall on Andy's right.

Brent shook his head, snapping out of the trance-like state everyone found themselves in watching Ben. The blond man shoved Andy aside and took a knee next to Willie.

"Hurt real bad," Willie said, lifting his large hand from a few deep cuts in his broad chest.

Brent took his time and inspected the wounds. For all his faults, the guy appeared to actually care about the men he commanded.

He placed a hand on Willie's bloody shoulder. "We'll get you fixed up, hermano."

Willie snorted, blood coloring his lips. "I don't even know what that means."

Brent patted his shoulder. "Means, brother."

"Oh," Willie said and smiled. "Okay."

Slowly, the bartender and regulars stood from behind the bar. They blinked at all the carnage and appeared to notice Andy and the team for the first time.

"Eh," Sully said. "Might need a bit'o bleach to get all this out."

Despite himself, Andy laughed.

CHAPTER 7

Willie's wounds weren't as life threatening as everyone thought.

A few stitches and he was good as new. Or, close to it. The doctor at the clinic said the big man could probably survive dozens of chupacabras before really getting hurt. Too much muscle mass to get through.

Chupacabras…

Of all the genetically spliced creatures roaming the world, the mythical ones were rarely ever "spotted". People had worse things to worry about than cryptids.

Or did they…?

The dead creature in the cantina wasn't a chupacabra, but the locals associated it with the legendary monster. Unusual things tended to get a bad rap anyway.

Ben skipped out on following the others to the clinic. Rather, he chose to haul the genetically spliced animal out of town and bury it.

"All they're going to do is chop it up and burn it," Ben told Brent before the rest of the team left the cantina. "They think it's something it's not."

"So, what are you going to do with it then?" Brent asked.

Ben sighed. "Take it out of town. Bury it."

"The fuckin' thing 'bout tore us apart and ya wanna—"

Ben loomed over Sully, a growl rumbling in his throat.

Sully held up his hands a bit and stepped back. "Whoa, big fella. Just be messin' with ya."

As they all piled into the Jeep to follow the bartender's truck with Willie howling in the back, Andy watched Ben lift the creature up and carry it on his broad shoulders. They rolled away before Andy could see which direction Ben chose to take.

Now, Andy was sat in the waiting room of a small, sweaty clinic for Willie to be discharged.

"He's gotta be the luckiest bastard I know," Sully said. He sat in the chair next to Andy.

"Yeah?" Andy turned a bit to look at the Irishman.

Sully smiled. He ran a hand through his black hair. "Aye. Was in his platoon six years ago now. Big bastard took a dozen bullets in that chest of his and still tore apart our enemies." Sully leaned close and whispered, "Literally with his bare hands. Right b'fore he fuckin' blew 'em to bits with his .50 cal." He winked. "Only had one bullet that made it close to his heary, ya know."

Andy blinked. "Really?"

"Yup." Sully stood. "The fecker's a machine."

"He almost died back then," Eldon said in a tone so soft, Andy barely heard him.

Sully huffed and again ran a hand through his hair. "Yeah, well, he didn't, right? 'Cause of all that muscles, the doc said."

"You mean," Eldon said, looking up from his tablet, "none of the shots were straight on, otherwise he would've been dead."

"Exactly," Sully said, pointing at Eldon. "Lucky bastard!"

Eldon sighed, shook his head and lowered it again.

"Y'gotta see 'em for what they're capable of," Sully told Andy, "not what they're thinkin'."

Andy nodded, not sure if he understood or not.

Sully tapped the side of his head. "Big bastards might not always be right upstairs, but they'll plow through anything."

Again, Andy nodded, still not sure if he understood the former. "Y'gotta see 'em for what they're capable of," Sully had said, "not what they're thinkin'."

What the hell did that even mean?

Andy let it go.

"Nice shootin', though," Sully said, giving Andy another nudge. "Aye. Good shootin'."

Les shuffled through the doors of the clinic, gave the team, minus Brent, Willie and Ben, a once over and plopped down next to Eldon. "Leave y'all for an hour and you're already in trouble."

Sully snorted. "Right. What a bunch'a goons they are."

Les rolled his eyes. "Where is everyone?"

"Brent said he had to make a few phone calls," Eldon said. "Willie is milking a few cuts and Ben went to go bury a genetically engineered animal."

Les opened his mouth, closed it and frowned. "Brent didn't say anything about an animal in his call."

Sully shrugged. "Bugger ain't he?"

Settling back in the chair a bit, the older man stroked his beard. "Wonder why he wanted me here? Thought we were gonna meet up at the hotel to get ready."

No one responded because, as far as Andy could tell, they didn't know the answer. Apparently, Brent was playing everything by ear now. Which was kind of unnerving, considering a mission like this needed careful planning. Maybe some intricate intel of the Cartel they're working for as well.

Working for...

Andy still hated the thought of working for any form of Cartel leader or lord, or whatever they were called now. Didn't matter. Because, big money or not, he was now a damn criminal. That alone he hated most of all. Being a criminal, when he became a Border Officer to help stop criminals. Not that all, or even most, come from the border. Not at all. Most of America's problems came from within.

But Andy wasn't able to pass the Police Academy because he couldn't run fast enough to beat the timer. He was never a good sprinter. Long distance, sure. No problem. But sprinting…

He failed, so he went to the next best option. A Border Officer with hopes to enter the Elite Patrol.

And now look where he was. Some cramped, sweaty clinic near the eastern edge of Tampico, Mexico.

"Okay," Brent said, striding into the waiting room. "Everything is ready to go. Wexler has the Echo Sub delivered and our other boss has the shipment ready."

Andy cringed at the mention of, "our other boss", and felt a bit better to notice Les doing the same. Eldon shook his head. The guy, Andy noted, was a hard read. Unlike Sully, who obviously went wherever the most action or money was promised.

"Right then," Sully said and jumped out of his chair. "Let's get the big bastard and be off."

Brent glanced around. "Willie hasn't been released yet?" Brent checked his phone. "We only got an hour to meet at the docks or the deal is off."

"Oh, Lord help us all if we're late," Les said. "May he strike us down for—"

"You don't get it," Brent said and approached Les. "If we don't make the deadline, we're all dead men."

Les's gray eyebrows knitted together in a deep frown. "You signed our death warrants then?" The older man stood. Brent was a good six inches taller, but that didn't appear to sway Les in the least. "Without telling us of the stakes?" The older man's frown deepened even more. "Who the fuck are you? Really?"

Brent drew his gun without further hesitation and planted the muzzle on Les's sunburned forehead. "I'm your *boss*, you fuckin' troll. Got that? If not, I can blow your brains out right here and now. If so, shut the fuck up and follow orders. Do you understand?"

Les's eyes shifted back and forth. Andy started to stand, but the older man left a staying hand at him. Sully patted Andy's shoulder in a weak gesture of comfort.

Brent pressed the pistol's muzzle harder on Les's forehead. "Do. You. Under-fucking-stand?"

"Yeah," Les said. "Wanna get the piece away from my head now?"

"Say it," Brent said. He was shaking now. "Say you understand."

The older man's glare never flinched. "I understand. Now get the fuckin' gun away from my head."

Yet, Brent lingered. Beads of sweat trickled down the sides of his face. He kept the pistol on Les's forehead. Andy reached for his own sidearm, ready to take Brent out before...

Finally, Brent lifted the gun, holstered it and said, "Good. I'll get Willie. Why don't you get that other oaf, Ben, eh, amigo? Took off west of town."

Les nodded, though didn't say anything.

Brent nodded back, turned and shoved through the double doors into the main clinic.

Les sagged a bit, and shook his head.

"Holy hell," Sully spouted. "Y'know he ain't right. Don't push 'im."

The older man waved a dismissive hand at the Irishman. "Shut up, ass licker."

"Hey," Sully began, but Les cut him off.

"Andy. Help me find Ben, okay?"

Andy stood, but Sully yanked on his arm.

"Boy'o ain't goin' nowhere, y'ol'bastard."

Les faced Sully. "You so up Brent's ass now, you can't let me make my own decisions? I figured Eldon is too busy thinkin', like always, and you're busy bein' a brown noser. So Andy would be the best choice. Now shut your paranoid Irish ass up and let me do what our *boss* wants me to do."

Sully blinked and didn't so much sit down as kind of gradually descend into the seat. Andy guessed the guy wasn't used to being talked to like that. Or being called a brown noser. Or, all the above. Probably all the above.

"C'mon, kid," Les said, turning Andy toward the doors. "Let's go find Big Ben."

CHAPTER 8

Andy didn't match Les's pace on purpose.

He hung back a little. The awkward silence was worse than a meandering conversation. Instead, he took in beautiful Tampico. The palm fronds rustling and waving in the sea breeze. Kids of all ages kicking a beat-up soccer ball around in one of the alleys. The gorgeously constructed and crafted buildings. Some of which towered over each other on their way toward the center of the city. Another sight Andy wouldn't mind experiencing.

Les kept to the outskirts, however. Perhaps to keep their profile as low as possible. Gringos stood out like a sore thumb. Not so much in cities like Tampico, but one never knew who was watching.

He didn't need to be a genius to note how everyone's gaze was drawn to Les and him as they made their way west. Just quick glances, but Andy couldn't but feel pinged. Maybe they were being tracked.

The thought stoked the coals of paranoia.

Yes. Yes, he felt watched. Someone was—

"You, me and Ben," Les said, cracking through the paranoia. "We're gonna have to stick together." He glanced over his broad shoulder. "Get up here so I don't look like I'm talkin' to myself, eh?"

Andy caught up to the older man, wiped away sweat with his forearm and said, "What do you mean?"

Les grunted. "Just as I said. We best stick together. I don't trust those other three. Eldon will go along with whatever Sully wants and Sully will kiss Brent's ass. I've worked with this lot before but they weren't so corrupt. At least, I don't think so."

They walked a bit more and Andy said, "How do you know I won't snitch you out to Brent?"

Les chuckled. "Well, if you do, I'll kill ya." He shot a bemused glance. "I know you won't, though."

"How?"

The older man shrugged. "I can tell you don't like Brent and I see how all this bothers you. Runnin' drugs isn't what you thought about when dreamin' of joining the Elite. So, now you're just goin' along with it for the money and hoping it all ends soon. Am I warm, kid?"

Andy sighed. "You're red hot. Yeah. I hate Brent. He tricked us all into this."

"Indeed," Les said. "He's got Willie too, I'm sure. Damn mongoloid wouldn't know right from wrong if it bit him on the dick. That's why you, me and Ben need to stick together. No tellin' what those assholes will try to pull." Les looked at Andy. "We watch each other's backs out there and after, okay?"

Andy nodded. "Okay."

Loose gravel crunched under their boots. Someone somewhere nearby strummed a guitar. The air smelled of sea salt, onions, cooking meat and motor oil. A strange and pungent conglomeration.

"Why don't any of us have phones or something?" Andy asked. "We could've called Ben."

Les laughed a little. "Probably don't want us free to call whoever and record whatever. Brent is a paranoid bastard."

Regardless, it didn't take as long as Andy thought it would to find Ben.

The man was sheen in sweat, his blue tank top dripping, when he stepped around a corner a few minutes after Les and Andy last spoke.

"Holy hell," Les said, surveying the big man. "We're in Mexico now, ya know. No marathon hay baling allowed."

Ben frowned, then smiled. "Made it through hotter summers in Iowa than this." His gaze drifted to Andy. "What are you two doing out and about?" He lingered on Andy for another couple of beats before his gaze shifted back to Les.

"Boss sent us to come looking for you."

Ben's frown returned. "Boss?"

"Brent," Les said. "He thinks he's in the mob or something now. Put a gun to my head when I stood up to him."

Ben straightened. "What?"

Les nodded, elbowed Andy. "Yup. Kid saw it too. He's with us."

Ben's cool gaze once more fell on Andy. "Us?"

"We go back longer than these fools, right? I trust you more than any of 'em. The kid here, he's a good one too. I figure it's best we stick close together. Just in case."

The big man didn't hesitate. "Agreed. I don't like what Brent signed us up for either."

"Money is good, but…" Les waved a hand. "Stinks like shit."

Ben chuckled. "Right."

They began walking back toward the clinic. From there they wouldn't stop at the hotel, like they should have, but go directly to the docks or harbor. Andy managed to get them to stop for a water before commencing their quick trek to the docks.

And so it went, Andy trying to chug a bottle of water while they figured out how to get to the east docks of Tampico.

"I'm from Iowa too," Andy told Ben. The view of the docks was maybe the length of a football field away.

Ben humphed. "Yeah? Heard that before? What town?"

"Manchester."

Ben snorted. "Yeah? Name the closest town."

"Depends, but I always thought Delhi or Ryan."

Ben's smile broadened. "Well, son of a bitch. I'm from around Ryan."

"You two done yankin' each other's pricks?" Les said, voice a low rumble. "They're waiting for us."

The docks, where Echo Sub 10 was to be deployed, weren't as large as those taking in the commercial liners and fishing boats. Indeed, the actual Port of Tampico was like a miniature town from where Andy and the team stood.

Brent was chatting with a man near the end of the longer of the docks.

With dusk settling in, the sky became a beautiful inferno of colors. Mostly pinks and purples, but not without its swaths of crimson. All those colors danced along the Gulf waters in all their sparkling splendor.

"'Bout fuckin' time, aye?" Sully said, grinning. His blue eyes shifted in their sockets, pausing on each of the three men, though lingering on Andy the longest. Then he looked at Ben. "Ya get to bury your pup?"

Ben nodded.

Sully clapped his hands together and tittered. "Why, that's good then!" In a blink, he glowered at the big man. "Get your gear on. We deploy in twenty." His glare fell on Les and Andy. "Same goes for you two."

Shaking his head and shoving by the Irishman, Les said, "Watch it, ya little Irish prick."

"The fuck ya say to me?"

The older man paused and faced Sully. "I said watch it, ya little Irish prick. Got a problem with that?" He gave Sully a withering look. "Last I checked, *you're* not my boss."

Sully's hands balled into tight fists. He started toward Les.

"That's enough," Andy said, stepping between them. "We're on the same side here, right?"

Barely audible, Les muttered, "The hell ya doin'?"

Andy ignored him and hoped no one else heard. "Right?"

Sully slumped a bit, sighed and gave Andy a firm nod. "Right. Sorry, ol' bugger. Might just be me nerves."

"Yeah," Les said, shooting Andy a look Andy couldn't read very well, and walked off, following Ben.

Willie loomed over Andy while Sully closed in.

The Irishman grinned. "Ya got some balls after all, eh?"

"Just think we should be working as a team and not at each other's throats. That's all." Andy began to turn away when Sully stopped him.

"Ya wanna make some extra money?"
Andy frowned.
Sully's grin lengthened.
The humorless grin of a snake.

CHAPTER 9

To Andy's surprise, the gear involved putting on the deep-sea suits. More like tight fitting mech suits, but whatever kept them alive if things went wrong down there. The helmets could be attached if needed.

Andy prayed there wouldn't be a need.

He had too much on his mind anyway. Too much to consider…

And, as they situated themselves in Echo Sub 10, he noted the kilos of what appeared to be cocaine stacked and filling up the rear where there should have been supplies. Like water and maybe some food. With all those kilos, however, there was not room for necessities. A few high caliber guns were present, though. For what purpose, Andy didn't know.

"Okay," Brent said, settling near the product. "It's gonna be a ride, but I promise you all, it'll be worth it." No one responded. "All we gotta do is assist the current convoy through the tunnels. Might need to create a shortcut near the center to catch up, but I think we'll be okay."

"Create a shortcut?" Andy asked, curious despite himself.

Brent's cold gaze found Andy. "I'll let everyone know when the time comes."

Andy nodded, trying to keep his anger at bay. If the sub wasn't already sealed and pressurizing, he might have jumped ship. Maybe he'd take out Brent if they came after him. Maybe not. Sometimes morals overrode intelligence. Regardless, he could see Brent on the docks with a smoldering bullet hole in his forehead.

"Prepare for dive," Sully shouted. "Buckle your shit and kiss your arses g'bye."

Across from Andy, Les rolled his head. Leaned in a gentle corner next to the older man, Ben snoozed away. Willie likewise snored in his own corner nearest the cockpit, bridge, whatever it was called. Where Eldon and Sully hung out, at any rate.

At least Brent was on Les's side so he didn't feel so sandwiched in.

"Locating Wormhole Nine," Eldon said. "Standby for further information."

"He always sounds so professional," Sully quipped. "But ya should see his search history…so weird."

Andy thought they were aiming for Wormhole Seven, according to their brief meeting with Angela Wexler. Where did the new instructions come from, and why wasn't the rest of the team informed upon arrival at the docks? It just led to further mistrust from Andy. In fact, he didn't trust anyone, except for Ben. Les, well, maybe a bit more than say, Sully or Brent. Ben just felt more genuine.

"Got a few shortfin Makos dartin' around," Sully said. "Haven't seen those in at least a decade."

Brent sighed. "Didn't bring you along for a species by species commentary, Sul. Shut your trap until you see something worth noting."

Sully, surprisingly, fell silent. A shame, really, because Andy could tell how excited the man was to see those Mako sharks. If nothing else, Sully loved sea life, apparently.

Andy leaned forward a bit so he could see out the curved windshield. He caught a glimpse of a few sharks and bunch of different fish but couldn't name any of them. They moved away too fast. Regardless, it was amazing. All blue with hints of mysterious gray the deeper they dove.

"Wormhole Nine is fifty feet below," Eldon said. "Descending now."

A gentle whoosh of air chilled Andy's sweaty face. He drew in a long breath, savoring it. Even if it was manufactured air, breathing under one hundred feet of ocean always gave him a bit of a thrill. It let him know he was alive. How technology would allow him to breathe underwater was amazing. A simple tank and flippers were enough to give him that feeling when he used to dive and not until now had he known how much he missed it. He—

"*Holy* shitballs," Sully shouted and nearly ran to the rear of the small sub.

"What?' Brent said, standing as best he could. Which was more of a slouch. The height of the sub wasn't much more than five feet.

"It was just an orca," Eldon said. "Sully is creaming his pants right now."

"Ya know how rare orcas are in these waters?" Sully's voice cracked like a prepubescent on the last word.

Everyone, even Les snickered.

"Shove it up all yer arses'n spin," Sully said. He gave Eldon a shove. "And you. Lucky I don't hit the fuckin' eject button and feed ya to that beautiful creature." He paused. "Eh, maybe not. Wouldn't want to get the poor thing sick. You bein' all sickly and whatnot."

"Hur-hur," Eldon said and shoved Sully back.

Sully punched Eldon's arm with a hearty *thwack*.

Eldon lunged at the Irishman.

"Oh, for fuck sake," Brent said and staggered to the front. He pushed them both back into their seats. "Knock it off. Christ, you're like a couple of toddlers with a toy." Brent growled and made his way to the seat near the rear of the sub, by all the cocaine.

A few seconds crawled by and Sully spouted, "See now? Ya made the boss mad. Ya fecker."

"*Me?*" Eldon said. "You started—"

"Shut up," Brent roared. "Or I swear to Christ I'll shoot you both in the head and drive this fucking thing myself."

Another handful of seconds went by.

"Probably shouldn't shoot a gun in a pressurized tube two hundred feet under the surface of the—"

"Eldon," Brent said, rubbing his temples. "One more word I won't care what happens to this sub or anyone on it. Just drive the damn thing and get us to where we need to go."

And, for a wonder, both Eldon and Sully fell silent.

Well, relatively.

A few minutes later, Eldon said, "Now entering Wormhole Nine. Switching to night vision and infrared."

"Turning proximity sensors on now," Sully said.

They both droned on like robots. All business now.

"Radio silence effective, n—"

"Echo Sub10," Angela Wexler said through the speakers, making everyone cringe. "Do you copy, Echo Sub 10?"

Brent sneered then blew out a sigh. He walked the cockpit and Sully tapped a flashing green phone icon on the panel.

"This is Echo Sub 10," Brent said, not even trying to sound interested. "What is it?"

"We have your location in Wormhole Five heading northeast. Can you tell me why you're not in Wormhole Seven, as agreed upon?"

Andy shot Les a glance. The older man shrugged. They were in Wormhole Nine. Not Five. Nothing made sense anymore.

"Eldon had a hunch about Five," Brent lied. "He thinks the runners are using that one the most. Said he thought he spotted a vessel near that location earlier. We're just going to check it out. If there's no evidence of another minisub, we'll turn back and go through Seven."

A long pause followed. "Okay." Wexler sounded more than a little confused. "Keep me updated, then."

"Will do. Thanks for checking in."

Click. The green phone icon winked out and turned red.

"See, El?" Sully said. "You're gettin' us in all kinds of trouble."

"Shut up," Eldon said.

"Both of you shut up and get this damn thing moving faster. We have a schedule, believe it or not." Brent sat back down in his seat.

"What happens when she realizes she's been made a fool?" Les asked.

Brent grunted, crossed his arms and leaned back. "She'll be pissed, but what can you do, right?"

"You'll throw us under the bus if comes to it," Andy said without thinking. It even garnered a look from Les.

Brent stared at Andy, face utterly expressionless. "Well, now…I'm sorry you feel that way, amigo. But I think you forget how much has already been deposited into your account. Three million dollars. You really think I would give that up so willingly if I wanted to throw you 'under the bus', as you put it?" He uncrossed his arms and leaned forward; steely glare fixed. Andy shivered. "No. Now, I know you're new and all, so I'll let it slide this time. But next time you have such a stupid comment froth up in that head of yours, bite your fucking tongue. Understand?"

And when Andy didn't reply right away…

"Do you understand?" Brent shouted.

"Yes," Andy said, keeping his voice as even as possible, though his heart rampaged in his chest.

Brent glared at him for a moment long, then nodded. "Good." He crossed his arms and leaned back in his seat again. His eyelids drooped shut. "We're a team now."

Andy looked at Les. The older man lowered his gaze and slightly shook his head. The older man didn't approve of Andy's comment, obviously. It wasn't like him to just spout off like that anyway. Maybe everything was finally sinking in. It's not that he thought he was a criminal now, but was, indeed one. He was willingly going along with it all.

Because of money.

Money that would give his kids a better life.

It always came down to money.

He supposed that's why Les and Ben were still in it too. Money was both a savior and a devil. It made people do the worst things just to obtain it. Wealth was part of the American dream, after all, right?

"Six hundred feet deep," Eldon said.

"Scrapings on the walls are fresh," Sully said. "We're in the right one."

With his eyes still closed, Brent said, "Good. Keep on until the fourth checkpoint. Wake me up when we get there."

Willie snorted awake, glanced around and wiped drool from his chin. "Fell asleep."

Ben sighed. "No shit."

Willie smiled and stretched, about smacking Les's head in the process. "We there yet?"

"No, you stupid oaf," Les said.

"Hey." Willie frowned at Les. "What'd I ever do to you?"

The older man chuckled. "Nothing. Sleep well, then?"

"I, uh…yeah. Sure." He smacked his lips and looked around. "Thirsty."

"I don't think we have any wa—" Andy began but…

"Case of water back here," Brent said. "You all should get some shuteye before we get to our destination. Last leg will be the part we need to pay attention to."

Les got up, pulled a bottle of water from the case and tossed it to Willie. The big guy guzzled it down in a couple of seconds and Les tossed him one more. To which Willie also guzzled empty. He crushed the biodegradable plastic composite bottle in his massive hand and let the remains plop on to the floor.

Les leaned back in his seat and yawned.

Ben whispered in Andy's ear. "We'll take shifts. You get sleep first. I'll wake you when I can't stay awake anymore."

Andy nodded, grateful. He hadn't realized how tired he really was until that moment. He leaned into his seat, which was like falling into a firm embrace.

He closed his eyes.

CHAPTER 10

"…up."

The world shook, rocking on the precipice of time. It tilted out of darkness. Tilted and tilted and—

"Wake up, man," Ben whispered in Andy's ear. "Shit just hit the fan."

Somewhere in the distance, an alarm brayed.

Andy flinched, waking up a bit, though stuck in a gray fog. Sluggish and weak, he struggled to wade through the muck of sleep into the real world. God, he was so tired. Too tired to move.

Might as well just close his eyes again and drift into oblivion.

"Andy," Ben said. Louder this time.

Andy sat up, breath caught in his throat like a rusty fishhook.

With a large hand on Andy's shoulder, Ben said, "Shh."

Brent sagged in the cockpit doorway shouting at either Eldon or Sully, or both. Probably both. "I don't fucking care if they came at us first, you do *not* engage! They probably didn't realize who we were at first."

"Feckers sure acted like they fuckin' did, man," Sully said. "The hell else we s'posed to do?"

"You hold your ground, that's what you do. And you most certainly do *not* fire back! Lucky for you, I have a direct link to their boss. Our *real* boss." Brent spun away, stormed to the rear of the sub and pulled out a phone.

He tapped it and held it to his ear. After a few seconds, he cringed, holding it away while another man shouted at him in angry Spanish.

Once the voice quieted, Brent put the phone back to ear and said, "Señor Guerra. Mi amigo! Listen, I—"

But Señor Guerra didn't sound like he was buying the mi amigo bullshit, from what Andy could hear rattling out the phone.

"How's that thing even working down here?" Andy asked himself.

"I assume, Ol'Guerra," Les said, "has been doing this for a while and has the best tech in the world."

"What happened anyway?" Andy asked.

"One of the other subs we're following rammed us," Ben said. "Sully shot at it with a blaster of some kind. He missed, but Brent went apeshit, as you can tell. Think our new boss is pissed too."

Les grunted. "What gave you that idea?"

Ben smiled.

"Have any of you heard of this Guerra?"

Les nodded but cocked a thumb at Sully who crouched in the cockpit doorway. The Irishman didn't appear to be paying attention to them, however. His focus narrowed on Brent.

"Yes, yes," Brent said when Guerra finally calmed down. "A pure mistake. My captain thought your vessel was trying to attack ours." Brent waited, nodded. His gaze drifted to Sully. "Yes. He'll be reprimanded. I assure you."

Sully blinked and melted back into the cockpit. "Fuck," he whispered.

"Of course, mi amigo," Brent said, all smiles and sweeping gestures. "We are right on schedule and will deviate from the convoy soon. I—" He moved the phone away from his ear and glared at it. "Well, fuck you too." He slipped the phone in his jeans pocket behind the deep-sea suit.

The suits, Andy came to realize, were pretty flexible considering they were more like a highly technological mech. There seemed to be some exoskeleton, though extremely lightweight. He wished they had had a chance to get used to them rather than a brief talk and a pat on the back for good luck. All the lab technician told him, other than the suits being the, "latest and greatest, m'man", was to follow the instructions once the helmet was secure.

"Pretty gnarly at first," said the young tech. "But you'll all be good. Just stay calm."

Now, glancing over his team of criminals, he wondered how they'd each react if they needed to use the suits?

Brent plopped down, leaned forward and rubbed his temples. "Stay the course. And don't shoot anyone this time."

Without a word from Eldon or Sully, Echo Sub 10 scooted onward.

Andy surveyed the team briefly. Just in case shit went nuts, he'd need a good idea on who to focus on first. His gaze lit on Willie. The big man picked a big green booger out of his nose, squinted at it like it was talking to him, and ate it.

Yeah. Willie would be the first one he'd need to calm down. That's if the big man managed to get his helmet on in time. The way he slouched it was a wonder he fit in the small sub at all. Indeed, he took up two seats width alone and the struggle to try and keep a behemoth like that calm might prove fatal.

Next would be Sully, or maybe even Brent. Though Sully seemed to be the most impatient of the two. Andy would have to assess the situation and go from there. He didn't think either would be much trouble.

Les, Ben and Eldon were all the calm ones of the group.

Still, Andy decided to speak up. They might all be criminals and Brent a giant douchecanoe, but they were also all in this together. Like it or not.

"We need to talk about the suits."

The entire minisub fell silent. Brent straightened, glowering at Andy. Les nodded. Willie ate another bright green booger. From the cockpit, Sully turned partially, dark eyebrow cocked. Eldon continued piloting the sub.

"Well?" Brent said. "What about the suits?"

"Okay," Andy said, trying to ignore the pressure of all eyes on him. The frantic beating of his heart defied him, however. "I—Okay, so if something bad happens. If we're losing pressure or taking on water. Anything like that—"

"Oh, for fuck sake," Sully spouted. "Spit'er out, boy."

Anger rose up in Andy like a cobra. Ready to strike. He turned enough to look at Sully. "I'm trying to save your goddamn life here. So, either you shut the hell up and listen, or I let you drown."

Now both the Irishman's dark eyebrows shot up.

Andy looked away, trying to involve everyone as much as possible. "If something happens—"

"It won't," Brent said.

Andy nodded, "*If* something happens, you need to know the basics."

Brent shook his head, though gestured for Andy to continue.

"You lock and seal the helmet by making sure the face is looking at your right shoulder. Press down and turn counterclockwise to lock and seal. When helmet and suit are linked, the visor will—"

"We're here," Eldon said, cutting Andy off.

Brent shot out of his seat and strode to the cockpit, ignoring Andy.

"Then what?" Ben asked.

Across the aisle, Les nodded.

"Once they're linked, there will be instructions on breathing and voice commands. You'll need to hold your breath for thirty seconds until the suit adjusts to you. When there's enough pressure and oxygen, you can voice command the suit's temperature, and many other things. Most importantly are the boosts in the palms and bottom of the boots. They're nothing fancy but will get you to where you need to go and recharge while they run. There are booster boosts, but you might want to only use those if in trouble. Once used, it takes approximately twenty seconds to recharge the capacitors."

No one said anything for at least five minutes.

"And you're absolutely sure?" Brent asked. "I don't think anyone trained you."

"Not one hundred percent," Andy admitted. "But the technician explained some of it. I'll have to play it by ear too."

"Oh," Sully said, "ain't that just a wet dream? You're gonna play'er by ear, aye?" The man swung back in his seat and faced the depths of the Gulf of Mexico. "Might as well hump a wall."

Andy ignored him. "It's better you know what to do before anything happens than—"

"Location acquired," Eldon said. "Awaiting further command."

Brent smiled, clapped his hands and surged to the cockpit door. "That rock. Yes, the red one. Shoot the blasters at it. If those don't work, use charges. We need to break into the next chamber. It'll bring us safely to Pensacola, Florida. Should be people there to help us out."

"That'll take almost nineteen hours," Eldon said.

"Put it on autopilot once we break through. Have Sully co-pilot and get some shut eye."

"What about me, ya arse?"

"Sul, you rest after Eldon. Just mark the same distance so you both get the same amount of sleep. I think it's a straight shot from where we are."

"Why are we separating ourselves from the others?" Les asked.

Brent shot a glare over his shoulder. "Because that's what we have to do. That's why we're getting paid so much."

And there it was. The money motivator. The singular thing which drove most people mad, even if just longing for it. Andy had seen plenty of his friends fall victim to the exploits of money and forget who they are. And, currently, he was one of the mad.

Did it matter if all he thought about were his children? No. He was still part of the Gulf Cartel, like it or not. They were paying him six million dollars, after all. That's a lot of money for someone who grew up in a small, poor, Iowa town. In a family who were grateful when they could afford ground beef, let alone new shoes for school. And most of the time those shoes were found at some secondhand shop or another.

Six million dollars was a mind-blowing amount for Andy.

It took several tries, but Sully and Eldon finally managed to blow a hole into the side of the tunnel where Brent wanted. Where the red rock stood.

Six charges later, with no collapses, thank God, they were on their way to Pensacola, Florida.

Still, Eldon stopped the sub and said, "This tunnel is wider, but we need to dive another eight hundred feet. Maybe more. The sensors are glitching a bit. At least eight hundred feet, though. That would put us over one thousand feet deep."

"Well, what are you waiting for?" Brent buckled into his harness. "The sub can handle way more than that. Let's go."

Andy caught Eldon shaking his head and the sub didn't move for another couple of minutes. Eventually, though, Echo Sub 10 began to tilt.

"Prepare for dive," Eldon said. "Buckle in."

Andy secured his harness and closed his eyes while the sub tilted, and vertigo churned his stomach. After a bit, though, his stomach and mind eased. His nerves settled.

Before he knew it, sleep stole him away once more.

CHAPTER 11

When Andy opened his eyes, he found only him, Sully and Brent were awake.

He sighed and sat up straight. The descent seemed to be over, so he unbuckled the harness. And when he swallowed, his throat gave a dry click.

He stood, legs a bit wobbly, and made his way toward the rear where Brent tapped away on his phone, ignoring everything else. Which was all well and good for Andy. The last thing he wanted was to have some awkward conversation with the man. All he needed was a bottle of water.

The single case of biodegradable plastic bottles rested to the left of all the cocaine. It was secured with a nylon strap to the floor. Andy didn't even have to loosen the strap. He weaseled a bottle out, opened it and drank about half before turning back toward his seat.

He managed two steps when Brent said, "Feeling okay?"

Andy stopped. The man appeared still focused on his phone.

"Yeah. Just thirsty."

Brent lowered the phone and frowned at Andy. The light in the minisub was dim, but enough to see clearly. Brent's expression was more than just a frown. Something in those cold, blue eyes held something more.

"I expected you to be more vocal than you've been, Andy," Brent said. "Good stuff about the suits, but other than that...you seem to be pretty chummy with Les."

Andy shrugged. "Things have been moving pretty fast. Guess I'm just catching up a bit."

Brent leaned forward. "You know your buddy, Les, gunned down an entire houseful of immigrant kids without investigating first? Yup. Just kicked down the door and tore through them all. Didn't even stop until they were all dead."

Andy lowered the bottle of water and faced Brent. "Maybe he didn't know they were kids." His gaze drifted to the older man asleep in his seat.

"Oh," Brent said and dropped the phone in his lap. "He knew. He just didn't care. This was years ago in Iran, but do you really wanna be buds with a man who could kill kids without a second thought?" Brent sighed. "I'm a father too and I know I wouldn't trust the bastard."

"You're a dad?" Andy asked, lost in bewilderment.

"Yup," Brent said. "Ten and sixteen. Both girls."

Andy, despite himself sat across from Brent. "So, why are you doing something like this? You could lose them if the Government found out. Not to mention you'd be in prison."

Brent chuckled. "Yeah, well, we all do crazy things for our kids, don't we?"

Andy nodded. That was true enough. Any parent worth their salt flipped over backwards for their children. Because kids were innocent and deserved everything good a parent could offer. No matter how little or much.

"Les ever talk about his kids?" Brent said, grinning a bit. "He ever mention grandkids?"

Andy thought about it and shook his head. "No." He wasn't quite connecting what Brent might be getting at.

"So," Brent said, "he doesn't know what it's like to have kids, does he?"

"No," Andy said, wondering what Brent's point was.

"He doesn't know what drives a parent, a dad, to do what we have to do to provide for our children. He has never known. The money means nothing to him." Brent paused, smiled. "He kills kids, Andy. He doesn't care."

Andy looked at Les. The older man snoozed away, oblivious. His big, bushy gray beard rose and fell with every mild snore.

"He isn't like us. Neither are any of them. Sully has a kid somewhere, but he never attempts to contact the poor child. They don't get our motivation."

"Heard that," Sully said.

Brent sighed and shook his head, ignoring the Irishman. "We need to stick together."

And, by God, he *believed* Brent. Andy could see himself partnering with the man and going on multiple "missions" through the years and slough it all off with the excuse it was all for their children.

But, did Brent really have kids? The guy could be lying through his teeth. And, if so, he was an incredible actor because Andy had a hard time detecting any lies. There was no looking up to the right, or fidgeting. Nothing.

"So," Andy said, "What should we do?"

Brent chuckled and leaned back. He closed his eyes. "For now, we sleep until we're there, hermano."

Andy stood, drank some more water and sat in his seat. His mind reeled. What if it wasn't Les he should be parenting with, but Brent? What if Les was the real villain? Any guy who could kill an innocent child was seriously fucked up in the head. And, if Brent was to be believed, Les was just that. A mad gunman who didn't care who died if they were over enemy lines.

Or was he?

Andy's gaze drifted to the older man once more. He appeared so grandfatherly, even in sleep. If not for the current setting, Les could be a sleepy grandpa snoozing away in a recliner after a long Christmas dinner. A jolly man, chuckling while the grandkids tore open their presents. Despite Les's rough exterior, Andy could see the jolly, happy grandpa. He could see the man laughing and hugging his grandchildren.

But what if Brent was right? The image of Les gunning down a houseful of kids splashed red over the image of the jolly grandfather, tainting everything in gray. Who was Les? Was he any different than Brent? Why did the older man want Andy to stick with him and Ben rather than integrate into the team?

Again, Andy's gaze fell on Les.

"Hey, boy-o," Sully whispered. "Come keep me some company, aye? Got cameras. I know you're awake."

Brent rolled away a bit, facing the kilos of cocaine. A snore buzzed from him. The guy must have been really tired to fall asleep so fast. A power nap, perhaps? God knew Andy had taken a few power naps at his post on the border. Sometimes that was needed. He even took two while on Echo Sub 10. The body and brain needed to just shut down sometimes.

Andy, despite his better judgement, crouched inside the doorway of the cockpit. "What?"

Sully didn't look at him, though Andy could tell the man was smiling by his profile. "Look out there, will ya?" He gestured at the windshield, or rather, what was beyond it.

Wormhole was a pretty spot on analogy. The tiny debris particles highlighted by the sub's high-density lights might as well be stars shooting by. The rocky walls were rifts through time and space. Indeed, it was like a whole new reality. One just as uncertain as the next. And in the distance lay the unrelenting darkness of the unknown.

"We're in the black water now, bud," Sully whispered.

Andy frowned. "Like Wexler's company?"

Sully snorted. "No, ya feck. This is the real black water. Where nothin' much can survive in these tunnels. Ever hear of a mad octopus? Only one I ever saw was in a sea tunnel like this, and that one was one 'bout forty meters down. Was stuck in the black water, though. No light. No food. Nothin'."

Andy stared out the curved windshield. He had always been a little claustrophobic, but now...now...

They were God knew how deep in the Gulf of Mexico under not only water but the ocean floor as well. One tiny earthquake could collapse the tunnel and, boom, everyone was dead. All at once, the walls of the tunnel seemed to be closing in. Eventually they would—

"Aye," Sully said, thankfully ripping Andy out his thoughts. "Bastard went mad the moment my light struck 'im. Swam right into me. Inked too. I couldn't even see m'willie. Next thing I know it's trying to hug my face like those things in that alien movie with Sigourney Weaver, ya know?"

Andy nodded. He watched the movies plenty of times growing up.

"Fucker wrapped around my head, sucked the respirator right outta m'mouth. Fuckin' beak cut my face up. I stabbed the fecker. Had too. Broke m'heart, but I had to. Stabbed it until I could pry it off." The Irishman shook his head and sighed. "That's what black water does. Drives ya mad."

A shiver trickled through Andy. He needed to look away from the darkness ahead. How long were they supposed to be in the damn tunnel? Nineteen hours? How long had it been? Were they even close?

Andy was about to open his mouth to ask Sully that when the man hissed, and the sub slowed. Andy blinked and looked out the windshield again. The sub stopped. Andy's eyes widened.

"Is that a...a..."

"Aye. Too deep for'er. Poor girl."

"What are you gonna do?"

"Only thing I *can* do, boy-o." Sully's tone dropped, like he was on the verge of sobbing. "Back to yer seat."

Andy shook his head, mesmerized by the large great white shark swimming down the tunnel toward them. Its nose was a shredded mess, and Andy soon discovered why. Every now and then it would bump into the ragged walls, tearing away more and more flesh. Its huge, toothy mouth snapped at nothing.

"She won't hurt us in here," Sully said. "She can't. But she will attack and kill herself doin' it." He leaned forward. "She already knows we're here..."

"So," Andy said, "what are you going to do?"

"Quick blast," Sully said and sighed. "Poor girl. I fuckin' hate when I gotta do somethin' like this." He shot a glare at Andy. Tears streamed down his face. "Get in your seat, ya feckin' idiot."

Andy didn't move. "I'm here for you, man."

Sully chuckled. "The fuck ya think I need someone? Get your arse in your seat."

Andy sighed and returned to his seat. Everyone around him snored. He leaned forward so he could see out the windshield through the cockpit doorway.

"G'bye, dear," Sully said and in the following second, a cloud of pink and gray filled the view.

Andy lowered his head. Great white sharks were scary, sure, but they were living things. They were just apex predators doing their thing and humans just happened to get in the way sometimes. As happened since the existence of man.

Eventually, the shark debris cleared and Sully continued the journey.

Andy sat back in his seat, sad for the shark. Sad for Sully. Because, despite his faults, the Irishman cared about life. Especially sea life.

A few minutes brushed by and Sully said, "Go to sleep."

But Andy didn't go to sleep.

CHAPTER 12

He sat there for hours, lost in his own mind when Sully said, "Get the fuck up." He gave Eldon a shove. "My turn to sleep."

Eldon snorted, sat up a bit and looked around. "Hours?"

"Ya been asleep for eight," Sully said. "We're fourteen in. Now wake up and get us there, ya fecker."

Eldon cleared his throat, and straightened. "Alright. Anything happen?"

"Had to blow apart a white shark."

"A great white? Down *here*?"

"Aye." Again, Sully's voice was low, and sorrowful. "Poor girl."

"That's very rare," Eldon said.

"Aye. It is." Sully rolled away in his seat. "Just get us there. Feckin' step on it."

Eldon didn't even look at Sully. Instead, Andy was forced back a bit while the minisub picked up speed.

Despite everything, Andy eased into his seat, though didn't fall asleep entirely. He dozed off and on. Not allowing himself to rest fully.

***

"Wake the fuck up!"

Beeping and the stench of smoke beat at Andy's face. He blinked, intending on ignoring it, when Les shouted, "We need ya, kid. Wake up!"

Andy woke, finding Echo Sub 10 in chaos.

Brent was barking at Eldon and Sully while Willie glanced around as though he was lost. Ben handed Les and Andy their helmets.

"What's going on?" Andy asked.

"Fuckers tricked us," Les shouted. "Get your helmet on. We're—"

Before Andy could so much as move, something struck the sub hard enough to knock Les off his feet and rock Andy in his seat. The beeping turned to braying. Hissing joined in all the noisy fun. The lighting dimmed red. The reek smoke got worse. Burning plastic.

Les stood, and helped Andy to his feet.

In the cockpit doorway, Brent roared into his phone. He screamed at Eldon and Sully.

"What the actual fuck, Guerra? *We* have *your* cargo! Tell your guys to knock it off or they'll sink us."

At Eldon and Sully, Brent shouted, "Hold your fire! Don't shoot them."

"Better figure somethin' out quick, *Boss*," Sully said. "Or I'm gonna blast 'em"

"We can't take much more," Eldon said. "We're in pretty bad shape."

"You just do your jobs and let me fucking think," Brent shouted. In the phone, he said, "Guerra. Mi amigo, tell your men to back off, por favor? I—" He looked at the phone and sneered. "Bastard hung up on me."

Another blast struck Echo Sub 10, sending everyone but Eldon and Sully stumbling. Andy wished Brent would move away from the doorway so he could see what was going on.

"That's it," Brent said. "Fire!"

"'Bout time," Sully said.

The sub rocked just enough for Brent to move. Directly in front of them and not far, was another small sub, only it looked like it had seen better days. The lights of Echo Sub 10 played off this other sub's dents and deep scratches.

Then it was nothing but an explosion of scarlet bubbles and sparks.

Then Brent blocked the view again.

Everyone on the sub stood silent for a few minutes while the alarms died off. Les plopped into his seat. Willie blinked at Brent while Ben held his helmet up as if inspecting it.

"We have a small fire here," Eldon said. "Sul, give me the extinguisher."

"Aye."

The whooshing of a fire extinguisher filled the sub. Brent turned away, coughing while Sully and Eldon were stuck in a white cloud in the cockpit.

After a moment, Sully muttered, "Idiot."

Eventually, the white cloud dissipated.

"How were they in this tunnel, anyway?" Les asked. "Thought we were taking a different route."

"Feckers set us up," Sully said.

Seconds droned on and Andy wasn't sure if he should move or even breathe.

"Are we okay?" Brent asked.

"No," Eldon said. "Sensors aren't working and some of our controls are fried."

Brent sighed. "Can we move?"

A long pause from Eldon. Finally, "Only forward. Reverse is shot. We can turn left and right, but I don't know about diving or ascending until we need to employ them."

"Alright," Brent said and sat in his seat by the kilos of cocaine. "Just…just get us out of here."

A man defeated, that was what Brent looked like to Andy. He slouched in the seat and glared at the phone in his hand. A defeated man, yes, but also a betrayed man. His employer wanted him taken out. Why? Only Brent and his employer would know that answer. Maybe Brent did something Guerra found suspicious or, probably, Guerra was done with Brent and just wanted to get rid of him.

The sub began to move again.

Andy's gaze fixed on the kilos of cocaine. He stood, drew the dagger from the right thigh of his suit and stood in front of the stacked kilos. A few had been skewed by all the blasts.

"The hell you doing?" Brent said and stood. "Sit back down."

Andy shook his head and stabbed the knife blade into the nearest block.

"You son of a—"

Brent crashed into Andy, driving him into the nearest wall. And, even though Andy wasn't trying to stab the man, Brent gripped the arm holding the knife. The blond man was taller, but Andy was stronger and shoved the man away.

"Stop," Andy said.

Brent roared and came at him low. On instinct, Andy kneed him in the face. The blond man dropped, howling and rolling on the floor of the sub. His hands clasped his face. Brent rolled away, his howls turning to cries of rage and pain.

"The hell's goin' on back there?" Sully said.

"Andy's *crazy*," Willie shouted. "He's hurtin' Brent."

"Stop'im, big boy," Sully said. "Can't have a nutball on this sub, right?"

"Okay," Willie said, and turned his full attention on Andy.

Andy gulped. "Willie. Look. I didn't mean to hurt—"

The giant man rose and stormed toward Andy. Les and Ben stopped him before he bashed Andy to a pulp.

"Stop," Ben shouted at Willie, straining to keep the massive man still. "Let's see what Andy has to say first."

"Has to say?" Sully said from the cockpit. "He just beat up our boss, right?"

"Our *boss* attacked him," Les said. "Andy was defending himself."

Sully fell silent.

Les made a hurry up gesture with his hand to Andy.

Back at the kilos of cocaine, Andy yanked the knife out of a brick and turned to the team. "When I worked at the border post, my mentor,

Genson, taught me how to know if a smuggler was really carrying cocaine or a decoy."

"The fuck ya on 'bout?" Sully shouted.

Andy licked his fingertip, tapped the hole in the cocaine and held his finger up with the off-white power covering the tip. "Looks like cocaine. Off white, almost pinkish, but it's really hard to tell in this light."

Climbing in his seat, blood drizzling from a crooked nose, Brent sat and glared at Andy.

"So, by the look," Andy continued, "this could be cocaine, alright. But, there's a test to really be sure."

Willie, not pushing to tear Andy's head off anymore, blinked. Rapt. "How?"

"Cocaine," Andy said, "will have a bitter, floral taste with hints of chemicals like kerosene or ammonia. It'll be more bitter than anything. And...it'll numb the gumline."

Without further hesitation, Andy popped his fingertip into his mouth and rubbed the power across the gumline of his front teeth.

Everyone stared, even Brent. The entire minisub sat in silence while Andy tested the cocaine.

He spat out a foamy, white substance, gagged, yanked free a bottle and swished water around in his mouth. He spat and swished again. The taste was awful. The worst thing in the world, but...

He spat once more and grimaced. In a choked voice, he managed, "That's not cocaine."

"Bullshit," Brent stood, voice wheezy and nasally. Blood still trickled over his chin and bibbed the front of him. "Guerra and I worked together for years. He wouldn't—" Brent dipped his finger in the cut Andy made and tasted the powder. A couple of seconds later he spat it out. Andy handed him the rest of his water to rinse with.

Andy looked at the team. "Looks like we're a decoy."

"Yeah," Ben said, "but decoy for what?"

Brent threw the empty bottle to the side. "We're not a fucking decoy. Bastard must've found a new American deal maker. I know too much." He glanced at the team. "This was all a setup. He planned to kill us."

"That's why the other sub kept shooting," Andy said.

"And why Guerra laughed in my ear and hung up," Brent said. He lowered his head. "He's not gonna let us out of these tunnels alive."

"Well, we took out the attacking sub," Sully said. "Should be fine, now, aye?"

"No. Six of his subs were deployed." Brent sat down and tried wiping the blood from his lips and chin. Instead it smeared into a joker's leering grin.

Andy tossed him a bottle of water. "Better clean up." He faced the team. Instincts taking over. Things Genson taught him. "Looks like we're in for a hell of a ride, then. We need to sneak by them somehow. Maybe tap into another tunnel system. And I think we shouldn't port at Pensacola."

A few seconds ticked by.

"Who the hell put *you* in charge?" Sully spouted. He stood and frowned through the cockpit doorway. "New guy."

Andy shook his head. "No one. And I'm not. I'm just saying, we need to figure something out here or they'll find us. I'm not sure how much more this sub can take."

"Not much," Eldon piped up. "That one sub hit us dead on six times with blasts and charges. The sub has shields, but those were gone after the fifth blast. That charge about got us if Sully and I hadn't reversed."

"How many more do you think we can take?" Andy asked.

"Two. Maye three more blasts. A charge will tear us open like a pop can."

"How much fuel do we have?" Andy asked.

"Still enough to make it to Pensacola, but beyond that, I'm not sure," Eldon said.

"Say we break into 'nother system, then," Sully said. "Where do we go?"

Andy had no idea, nor if Guerra had set up guards to take them out at every port. It was a crapshoot either way.

"Brownsville, Texas, maybe?"

Everyone fell silent for a moment.

"We'll aim for anywhere besides Florida," Brent said. "He'll be more focused there."

Andy nodded. "Right."

"Brownsville is too big," Brent said. "We need a smaller port."

Andy thought about it, though came up with nothing. He didn't know too many towns, only larger cities.

Les snapped his fingers. "Port Aransas. It's smaller. Might be a bit touristy, but…"

Brent, using the water to rinse his blood smeared face off, pointed at Les. "That might work. Set course for Port Aransas, El."

"Okay," Eldon said. Then, after about a minute, "Our sensors are too messed up, but it looks like we need to go to a deeper system below us and cut into an adjacent tunnel leading northwest from where we are."

"Do it," Brent said, using the collar of his shirt to wipe away the mess on his face the best he could, which helped to eliminate the creepy, bloody grin.

Sully frowned, glanced at Andy, and ducked back into his seat. Not long after, Echo Sub 10 began to move.

CHAPTER 13

"What about Wexler?" Ben asked while Eldon and Sully blasted into the deeper tunnel system.

Brent shook his head. "If she ever found out we were working for Guerra, she'd shut this sub down. They have external power to do so. She'd shut us down and we'd suffocate in here."

"We have the suits," Andy said. "They filter water into oxygen. We'd be okay as long as there weren't any predators around."

"Like a damn orca," Sully spouted. "Bastards think you're edible…you're fucked."

"They're rare, though, right?" Andy asked.

"In these waters? Aye. I saw one, though. They're out there."

"So," Brent said, "we avoid the suits. Just get us as close to Port Aransas without confrontation. We'll figure everything else out when we get there." He pinched the bridge of his nose and leaned back. Dried blood crushed around his nostrils.

Sully said, "Aye."

Eldon didn't say anything, and Andy assumed he was planning a course of action while they blasted through the rock to the deeper system. Eldon was smart and read things well. If anyone could truly get them out of this, it was him. Andy knew just by observing the guy. He kind of reminded Andy of Egon from Ghostbusters. No nonsense. Factual. Maybe even a bit mischievous.

Andy picked his helmet up, sat and turned it around over and over in his lap. Les, Willie and Ben sat too. No one said anything. No one needed to. They were a target. Now more than ever, once Guerra found out his people sent to kill them were dead. Were they carrying fake cocaine too? Just as an off chance their mission was compromised?

Yes, Andy thought. *This isn't a run…this is an assassination mission. Guerra is tying up loose ends. We need to—*

A blast rocked the small sub.

"Holy *shit*," Sully spouted. "Hold on everyone. Got a PTS."

"A *what*?" Brent called.

"Pressurized tunnel system," Sully said. "Means there were pockets'o'air." He grunted. "Not anymore."

"Is it dangerous?" Andy asked.

"Nah. We just gotta let'er blow for a bit."

"Reversing away from the air stream," Eldon said. "The release might take a while."

"That's what she said," Sully spouted and giggled.

Andy smiled, shook his head and looked at Les. What Brent told him never left his mind.

"Tell me what happened with the kids in the house?"

The older man blinked. "What are you talkin' about?" His squinty eyes also told Andy to lay off. But Andy wouldn't lay off. He needed to know.

"The house with all the immigrant kids. Did you really gun them down?"

From the corner of Andy's vision, Brent leaned forward. The tension in the sub became suffocating.

Les didn't break eye contact. "Brent didn't tell you the whole truth. Did you, Brent?"

Voice still nasally, Brent said, "You were told to investigate. Instead, you broke down the door and opened fire."

"You're a fuckin' liar," Les said and turned toward Brent. "*You* had *Sully* kill those kids. I tried to tell you there were kids in there!"

Brent glared at Les for a long time. From the cockpit, Sully chuckled humorlessly.

"Was told they were drug runners. All adults hidin' out, ya fecker."

Brent squirmed a bit in his seat, and glanced away from Andy. "I told you to take down the runners, not the kids."

Andy frowned. "You lied. Again."

"Course he lied," Sully said. "What the fecker does best. For the record, I didn't know kiddos were in that house. I should've checked, but he was my boss. I...I...I'm sorry." A bunch of quiet sniffles came from the cockpit.

"I have four grandchildren," Les said. "I wouldn't hurt a child."

"You were drunk," Brent said and laughed. "I told you to check the house first but you just—"

"It was me, areshole," Sully shouted. "You fuckin' sent me in there and it was so fuckin' dark I didn't know what was what, or who. You said they were all *men*, you *fuck*."

"We're not getting paid now, are we," Andy said. Not a question.

Brent never lifted his head. "No."

"You mother*fucker*," Sully shouted. "What about the money deposited into our accounts?"

Head still lowered, Brent said, "I doubt Guerra transferred anything."

A few ticks of quiet and—

Another blast struck the sub, this one hard enough to make Les vomit from all the spinning.

Once everything stilled, Eldon said, "They found us."

"Fire," Brent screamed, all wild eyed. He shot out of his seat and stormed to the cockpit. "Kill 'em all!"

Another strong blast rocked Echo Sub 10. Andy put the helmet on, ready to turn and engage it, but…

They didn't appear to be taking on any water and Sully shouted, "Got the fecker!"

"Diving into the new tunnel system," Eldon said. Calm, as though they weren't just attacked. Like nothing remotely wrong was going on.

Andy took off his helmet and leaned forward some so he could see out the windshield. They passed through a ragged hole into dark waters. If they were in "black water" before, as Sully put it, then this was obsidian water, or something like that. Somehow even darker. The walls were smoother too, by the look.

"It's natural," Sully said.

"What?" Eldon said, sounding more distracted than anything.

"The tunnels we were in above," Sully said, "they had ragged walls, most of 'em, except the one we just came from. This…I mean, *look*, man. The walls *flow*, they're so smooth."

"Okay?"

Sully sighed. "Means this tunnel has been here for a very long time, arsehole."

"Oh."

"It's a big one too," Sully continued. "Like a cave that goes on forever. Interesting."

"Sure."

Sully punched Eldon in the arm.

"Hey, what the *hell*?" Eldon rubbed his arm and shot a glare at the Irishman.

"Oh! Ya are human! Praise the Lord! 'Bout time ya didn't sound like a fuckin' robot."

Eldon turned back to piloting the sub and shook his head. "You really are a bastard, you know."

"Aye," Sully said, and chuckled. "Be the best damn bastard ya ever met too!"

Andy leaned back in his seat, mind reeling. So, they were in a natural, presumably, undiscovered tunnel perhaps thousands of feet below the surface of the Gulf of Mexico. Where did the tunnel lead? If Guerra's men were waiting above…where was Echo Sub 10 supposed to go to avoid all of them? Especially with most of the sensors down? Andy's heart stuttered at the thought. A sudden, terrified thought crossed his mind.

"How much air do we have left?"

The silence rolled out for so long, he was sure nobody heard him. He opened his mouth to repeat the question when Eldon said, "The Echo Sub 10 filters water through influx capacitors, generating oxygen. As long as we're moving, it produces air to breathe."

"Like a great white," Sully added. "They need to keep moving or they suffocate."

"Thanks," Eldon said, "for that useless informat—"

A massive boom quaked the minisub. A force so strong, it flung Andy out of his seat. He scrambled back to his seat, clutched his helmet and glanced at the others. All of them stared at him. Well, except for Willie, who was picking his nose again, and Eldon and Sully. Those two were too enthralled with trying to keep the sub from imploding, or whatever happened when a sub blew underwater. Didn't matter. They appeared to be following his lead now. Even Brent.

Loud hissing erupted through the sub.

"We've been breached," Eldon said.

"Suit up," Andy said without thought. "Make sure your suit is in the correct position and put your helmet on. Remember, you have to start with the right side and turn the helmet to activate and seal the suit." It was all he could remember and hoped it was all correct. Otherwise, they'd all be dead soon.

He stood and showed them how to turn the helmet from right to left. It sealed directly at center. Everyone appeared to get it, except for Willie, who went from the middle to the right. Andy helped the big man get the helmet locked down. Eldon and Sully locked their helmets on and the link was complete.

Mellow beeping. Words on the upper right of the visor read: Link Upload Complete. Initiating body scan.

"Can you all hear me?" Andy asked.

"Aye," Sully spouted. "This is cool. And we'll be fine in these depths?"

"That's what Wexler's tech said."

The mellow beeping changed to a series of high-pitched beeps before silence filled the helmet. The only sound was Andy's breathing until a light hiss and cool air whooshed around his face.

The words on the visor read: Regulating Temperature.

A few seconds later and the inside of the suit was a nice seventy degrees.

Andy turned, noting the water in the sub was already up to his knees. He stared at the ladder near the kilos of fake cocaine and the hatch above for a bit, then faced Les, not Brent.

"Once we open the hatch, we'll be flooded instantly."

"We'll implode," Eldon said. "Won't matter if we're wearing the suits or not. It'll kill us."

"So," Brent said. "What do we do?"

"I need to depressurize the sub."

"Do it," Andy said.

"Wait," Brent said. "Why can't we just patch the hole?"

"Did we happen to pack some metal and a welder?" Ben said. "If so, I can do it."

No one said anything for a short period of time. Eventually, everyone turned to Brent. The man, even in his suit, ruffled a bit.

"Hey, how the hell was I supposed to know this would happen? It was supposed to be an easy run."

"You didn't bring a small welder," Eldon said, "just in case?"

"Sorry to fucking disappoint you, Eldon, but no. I had other shit on my mind, is that okay with you?"

"Not really," Eldon said. "This sub should be relatively safe. Patching equipment is a must for all submersibles."

"Well, excuse the hell outta me," Brent said.

"We're supposed to be a team, right?" Andy said. "Well, let's act like it. Because that's the only way we're getting out of this. And, before Eldon shuts the pressure off, I want to go over a few—"

A loud explosion tore through Echo Sub 10, sending it spinning.

"Initializing balance control," the suit told Andy.

He blinked, then gaped when he wasn't tossed around inside the sub. The entire team didn't move from where they stood. No swaying. Nothing. It was as if they were temporary statues. Stoic. Unmovable. No matter how much the minisub rolled and jostled, no one moved from their spot.

"Damn," Les said. "These things are amazing."

"Don't cream your suit, Gramps," Sully said. "We're sure as dead soon as we leave the sub. Feckers will unload on us all. Y'know they're just waitin' out there to pick us off now."

Andy frowned. Sully was probably right. Guerra's men were set to kill anything and everything. Also, one more hit and the sub would either explode or implode. Either way would be bad.

He gave the others a quick glance. "Do we have any weapons?"

"Three self-contained carbines," Brent said. "Specially designed for underwater. Six M4 carbines for regular use. Everyone is carrying a pistol…"

Andy sighed. "The M4s are useless down here. The underwater carbines are useless against a sub." He moved to the rear of Echo Sub 10. Water streamed in from a missing rivet, or bolt. The pressure outside the sub would eventually crumple the sub like a pop can. "If we had an explosive, or something, maybe we could stop them."

"We don't," Brent said. "Wasn't like I *knew* I was going to get fucked over, ya know?"

A few other bolts near the one spewing water rattled, working their way out.

"We need to get out of here," Andy said. "Or we're all going to die."

"Depressurizing now," Eldon said through the helmet speakers. "At seventy percent and falling. I can't go below fifty percent, or we'll be crushed. We'll have to take our chances exiting."

"Okay," Andy said. "So, as soon as—"

"Look, Andy," Brent said and sloshed to the center of the minisub, "I know you're trying to help, but you forget who the boss is here."

Andy faced the man. "Are you really going to pull the Boss Card right now?"

"The hell you talking about?" Brent said. "I don't *need* a card. I *am* the boss."

"You got us into this shit," Les said. "Andy is tryin' to get us out."

"I *know* these people," Brent said. "I just need to talk to Guerra and—"

"He hung up on you, aye?" Sully spouted out of nowhere. "We're cut off, man. Let Andy do his thing."

Brent pointed at Andy. "This...*guy*? He's new. How can you even trust him?"

"Well," Ben said. "He didn't load us up with fake cocaine and send us out into the depths of a tunnel system under the Gulf of Mexico. There's that."

"Not to mention the fact you've fucked us over before," Les said. "Just not so badly as now."

"I have *never*—"

"Remember Syria?" Eldon said. "You told us we were meeting up with another team to take down some bad guys. Instead, they were a small militia hellbent on killing anyone who didn't believe in their political views."

"Look, I thought they were—"

"Or," Sully said, "the time when you were all giddy about that guns deal and ya almost got us fuckin' killed in London?"

"Well, remember I tried to—"

"If we hadn't gotten paid for those," Les said, "we wouldn't be here now. You understand? You're a piss poor leader and we followed only because of the money. God knows, if not for how much you paid us this time, we would have bugged out."

Brent turned to Les. "You fuckin' liar. You would've stayed anyway because you're too old for anything else beside a goddamn store greeter and you know it."

"Not if I knew I wasn't getting paid, which, apparently is the case now. You don't know shit about deep diving, Andy does. He's my leader for now."

"For now..." Brent lowered his head. "And when he gets you all killed?"

"Okay," Sully said and emerged from the cockpit. "So, what do you want us to do, *boss*?"

Brent flapped his arms in a seemingly exasperated gesture. "See if we can patch the hole and keep moving. I think that's safer than swimming around in these suits with no direction."

"The suits," Andy said, "have a navigation system. We should be okay as long as we avoid predators and the Cartel."

"And the Cartel are out there right now, dumbass," Brent said. "If we can patch the hole and get moving, we should be okay."

"Our depth is around two thousand feet," Eldon said. "It'll take more than a cotton ball to stop the leak. The sub's external sensors might be off, but the internal ones are still working. The sub is nearly sixty percent depressurized. It's not going to take long before we're crushed in here if we don't move soon."

"Well, we wouldn't be worrying about pressure if Andy hadn't—"

Then all Andy knew was a wall of silvery bubbles and darkness.

CHAPTER 14

"Stabilizing," a monotone voice said.

Andy's eyelids fluttered.

"Stabilized. Current depth, two thousand and eighty feet."

Andy groaned, his eyes opening to stare directly into a dark void. He blinked, and flailed for a moment, realizing he was floating, not standing.

"Do you wish to engage night vision?" the monotone voice asked. A pause. "Do you wish to engage night vision?" Pause. "Do you wish to—"

"Yes," Andy muttered and squinted when the visor turned goblin green and melded into real clarity with colors. It was weird seeing in the dark with such depth and clarity.

"Elite night vision engaged," the monotone voice of the suit said.

Elite...

Andy almost forgot he was wearing an Elite Patrol dive suit. He almost forgot who he really worked for.

Angela Wexler.

Brent must have cut all communications off because Wexler hadn't said anything since questioning why the team took a different tunnel. And, surely, she had some kind of tracking device built into the sub. It was an expensive piece of equipment. She wouldn't let it go without some way to keep an eye on it. At least that's the way Andy saw it. Wexler appeared to be the kind of person always in control.

Maybe, after everything, she'd have them all arrested. At the very least they'd probably be tortured. Or just tortured and hung upside down in a vat of tiger sharks.

But, first thing was first...they needed to hide from Guerra's men, get the hell out of the tunnels, and somehow make it to shore without getting chomped up by something. Didn't matter where. Just out of the damn water.

A voice shivered through the speakers in his helmet. "H-Hello?"

Andy shook his head and glanced around. The night vison wasn't the total goblin green kind, but instead, something clear as daylight. There was a green hue to everything, though nothing overt or too distracting. He gaped through black water without the slightest light and noted every swirl in the tunnel walls by, perhaps, centuries of erosion, in exquisite detail. He blinked at bobbing debris in front of him and—

The dark figure shot around a section of rock in front of Andy and surged toward him.

"Whoa," Andy said, shifting to the side and catching the man before he crashed into one of those beautifully smooth walls.

From the boots of the suit, bubbles shot out.

"Tell it to stop boosts," Andy told the man.

"Stop," Brent cried. "For fuck sake, stop boosts!"

The jet of bubbles ceased, and Andy was able to get Brent floating upright before the guy said, "We're so fucked, man."

"No," Andy said. "We'll be okay. Just need to keep our heads. Where's everyone else?"

"Don't know," Brent said. "Blast might've killed them."

Andy looked away, though doubted it. The rest of the team was still out there. Below, on the bottom of the giant tunnel, were the remains of Echo Sub 10. The particles and debris he squinted through was probably the fake coke and whatever else was in the sub.

There were no signs of bodies, or even pieces of them.

"Can anyone else hear me?" Andy called.

Only Brent's breathing greeted him.

Unless the others were completely obliterated, they were drifting around in the tunnels, unconscious. Which posed a very serious problem.

"They're dead," Brent said. "They're dead. We should go."

"No," Andy said. He positioned Brent so they were face to face, and he could see Brent's shocked face through the helmet's visor. "We're gonna find them."

"We can't," Brent shouted. "They're in pieces everywhere and—"

"Shut the fuck up."

Brent sucked in a breath but said nothing more.

Andy, heart thrumming, spared another glance around. "We need to find them."

"How?"

Andy pushed Brent away and turned from left to right. Beyond the reach of the colorful night vision lay only darkness either way. He frowned straight ahead at the large rock Brent had blasted around. There appeared to be yet another tunnel trailing off in that direction. Or, maybe, it was just a trick of the eye.

Only one way to find out.

"Engage low boost," he told the suit.

A gentle whir filled his helmet and millions of tiny, silvery bubbles encased him for a second or two. Before he could really wrap his mind around it, he was already drifting round the large rock and scooting steadily toward the mouth of a different tunnel.

"Hey," Brent said. "Where the hell are you going?"

"Checking this other tunnel out quick," Andy said, though he hadn't really planned on going in there alone. Probably for the best, though. Still…

"You can come along, if you want."

Brent didn't say anything for a couple of heartbeats. "I should stay here. Just in case they're in this tunnel."

Andy smiled, shook his head, while the suit propelled him slowly toward the tunnel. He somehow figured Brent would say just that.

"Good idea," Andy said. The last thing he wanted was Brent muddling his thoughts while he tried to search the tunnel. "Keep calling for them. Try different frequencies and channels. Like one of those old CB radios. Tell the suit what you want to do, and you shouldn't have a problem. Keep an eye out for Guerra's men too."

"You don't tell *me* what to do," Brent spouted. His voice was on the edge of growling.

Andy rolled his eyes and entered the tunnel. It was a lot narrower than the main tunnel. A tributary, perhaps. He decided to let Brent's comment drown. No use kicking up an argument. It'd get them nowhere and Brent would likely freak out and do something stupid. Luckily, the suits weren't equipped with weapons.

Weapons.

"Stop." The suit glided to a stop. "Brent, you copy?"

"What?"

Andy sighed and tried to ignore the man's crass reply. "Look for those submersible guns you were talking about. We might need them."

When Brent didn't say anything, Andy sighed and added, "Please?"

"Fine."

The narrow tunnel stretched on into bleak darkness in front of Andy. A watery pathway into Hell itself for all he knew. And still, he continued. Every now and then, Brent would call for the missing members of the team on the main frequency before telling his suit to switch to a different channel.

At least the guy was doing something. Even if Andy had ordered him to do it and he didn't like it. Maybe Brent cared for things after all. Maybe he wasn't just some cold, international drug dealer, but human.

Or, perhaps, Andy was giving the guy too much credit, but who knew?

Andy drifted down the tunnel. Like the main one, its walls were eroded smooth. He could almost see the centuries flowing across the stone, leaving its lines and swirls along the way. Browns and whites, yellows and reds. The stone of the tunnels were quite beautiful. All layered on top of each other and seen, perhaps, for the first time with human eyes.

He ventured about three hundred feet down the tunnel before giving up and heading back. Even if the team woke up before him and Brent, why would they go exploring right away? Didn't make any sense.

Still, he needed to be sure. If they really had ventured away, he couldn't help them right now.

When Andy emerged from the narrow tunnel into the main one, he found Brent on the tunnel's floor, picking through the sub's rubble.

"End boost," Andy said. He lowered in front of Brent as the jets in his boots subsided. "Anyone answer?"

"Nope," Brent said, sifting through some curled metal. "Not a damn peep."

Andy turned away. "Where did they go...?"

"Maybe they got caught in some current?"

Andy shook his head. "There's hardly a current. At most, they would've drifted maybe a couple hundred feet." He blinked. "How long were we out?"

"I don't know," Brent said.

The remains of Echo Sub 10 lay strewn along the floor of the tunnel. Twisted metal. Ragged sections of seats. How they even survived the blast was beyond Andy. Which gave him pause. What if only him and Brent survived? But, if so...where were the body parts and everything else? The broken kilos of fake cocaine created ghostly white clouds from where they rested on the floor among the other debris. But, from what Andy could tell, there was no blood. No floating limbs. No evidence whatsoever the team was dead. So, unless they were completely obliterated, they had to be around somewhere.

"Les?" Andy called. "Sully? Anyone copy?"

"I do," Brent said.

A breath too heavy to be a sigh blew out of Andy. "No shit, jackass." The words just rolled out of his mouth.

"Fuck you," Brent spat.

The problem with Brent, the guy was used to being in control. Regardless if he worked with someone else, he loved the control over his team. He reveled in changing plans and ordering people around, right or wrong. Being an asshole, in other words. But a guy like him didn't care, unless something was in it for him personally. Or, rather, financially.

The two men floated in silence for a few seconds while Andy's mind reeled.

"Hey," Brent said and swam down a bit to the wreckage.

"What?" Andy's heart stuttered. "What is it?" He imagined a severed head, or a hand, or...

Brent grunted and lifted aside a large section of metal. The moment before he let it fall and stirred up sand, Andy noticed a long, green rectangular box. A massive plume of sand and silt obscured everything for a while. Andy backed away, trying to control his breathing. It wasn't like he was in a tight space, but not able to see anything but gray sand and dark silt, unnerved him. Anything could be lurking in it. Anything at all.

Finally, the gritty cloud sifted to the floor. Brent floated next to the green box and flipped open four clasps.

"What's that?" Andy asked.

"Something that'll make us both feel better." Brent opened the box.

A few bubbles billowed out. Andy waved his arms to lower himself a bit more and blinked. "Are those—"

"The submersible assault rifles," Brent said. "Yup." He turned slowly. "Should be an ammo crate somewhere too."

Andy helped Brent sift through the wreckage until they found a deep, square box in the same deep shade of green.

"There we go," Brent said. He almost sounded like he might be drooling. All slurpy.

Things were moving fast now. Scary fast. Now there were guns in the picture. Guns with ammo. What would stop Brent from shooting everyone when—

"Help," a weak voice shivered through Andy's helmet.

Andy spun. "Hello? Who is this?"

A pause, then, "Ben."

"Holy shit," Brent said. "Where the fuck did you all go?"

Andy sighed. "Is everyone okay? Can you describe where you are?"

Another pause. "I don't know. Woke up in a chamber or cave. We're all here, except for you and Brent. I think I'm the only one awake."

"How the fuck did you all get so far away from us?" Brent asked. His tone was brash and unwarranted.

Andy closed his eyes, fighting the urge to grab a gun, load it and put a bullet through Brent's visor. The man was grotesque in far too many ways. Cold and fake.

"I—I don't know. Everything went white and the next thing I knew I was piled with everyone else in here."

Down the tunnel revealed only bleak darkness. Up the tunnel was the same. The improved night vision didn't clear anything after about fifty feet. Which direction would they have fallen victim to? There wasn't much of a current, but Andy decided to set his suit on detection mode, which gave him an idea of the environment he floated in. Better to get a heads up than nothing at all, he reckoned.

The suit soon relayed the information he needed and displayed it on the helmet visor.

CURRENT: 4 knots. Increased to 8 knots ten meters north. Minimal debris. LIFEFORMS DETECTED: 7.

Andy turned to Brent…and froze. The man pointed one of the submersible guns at him.

"What…?"

Brent grunted. "Thought you could just take over my operation, did ya? Mr. Big Leader? You're nothing but an Elite wannabe."

"I don't know what you're talking about."

"I'm the boss," Brent cried. "*Me*. Not you. That's *my* team out there. Not yours."

"I never claimed they were," Andy said. "I'm just trying to help."

"You're probably a Guerra rat. Got a tracking beacon on you or something, right? He knows where we are all the time. How? Huh? How does he know?"

"I don't—"

"Because of you! You're leading him to us. I should've known you'd be a rat. New guy Wexler picked off the fucking street, you don't know shit."

Andy frowned. "Are you having a stroke or something? You're—"

It darted from the darkness behind Brent and clamped down over the top half of his body. Brent screamed, fired a shot from the submersible rifle. Andy ordered the suit to boost away, but thankfully the round went wild.

In his ears, Brent continued to scream.

Blood clouded and obscured Andy's sight of the man and his attacker. All Andy could remember was the massive, darting mouth full of teeth. Long, needlelike teeth. And that was enough to stoke terror through him.

"Medium boost," he ordered the suit. It shot him backward, away from the massive red cloud.

Brent's screams turned garbled.

"W-What's going on?" Ben asked. "Someone screamed."

Andy couldn't answer him. It took all his will not to scream himself.

Eventually, Brent's screams stopped.

Andy hid behind the large rock dividing the main tunnel from the smaller one. The splitting of channels, perhaps? A divide between the majority and the minority.

He peered around the rock in time to watch Brent be sucked into a large, dark gray creature with a long snout. Before he could really note any more features, the thing surged forward down the tunnel. A massive wall of moving gray, which took at least three minutes to pass by, struck Andy with the deepest fear he'd ever known.

He rolled away behind the rock, trying to control his breathing.

What the hell was down here with them?

Whatever it was, the thing was huge. Thirty feet long, at least. Probably more.

Did another great white find its way down here? There was that one Sully killed not long ago, but it hadn't been this deep. Over two thousand feet, last Andy knew. Not too deep for a great white, though having one stalking the tunnels…like Sully said, it was beyond rare. But sometimes aquatic life found itself trapped. Rare, but it happened.

Andy made many deep dives, but there was always the nagging strain at the back of his mind. That gnawing fear a big shark would just dart in and chomp him in half like a cheap sardine was all too palpable.

Heart thrumming, he opened his mouth to warn Ben about the creature, but all that came out was a long wheeze. He groaned and tried again.

"Big," he managed.

"What? Andy? Is that you? Say again."

Andy wetted his lips, cleared his throat. "Big creature just ate Brent." It all came tumbling out.

A slight pause, then Sully said, "What kind'o creature ya talkin' 'bout?"

"I…I don't know. It was big. At least thirty feet long. Maybe more. Its mouth *shot out* and grabbed Brent."

"Shot out," Sully mused. "Aye."

"Do you see it?" Andy asked.

"No," Ben said. "Our tunnel is clear."

So, that eliminated the main tunnel the creature moved through. Good. Where the hell were they then?

He didn't know if it would work, but Andy had to try. "Pinpoint lifeforms."

Green text blipped on the visor: COMMAND NOT RECOGNIZED.

Andy sighed and gave it another shot. "Locate lifeforms."

His helmet beeped. The words across the visor read: LOCATING…

Andy peered around the rock to make sure the large creature was gone and swam to the box of guns. He picked one up, drifted to the ammo box, and jacked in a fresh magazine. The suit's fingers were thick and difficult to move with any amount of dexterity, but he managed to wriggle his right index finger over the trigger.

"I have guns," Andy said. "Soon as the suit locates you, I'll bring you to them."

"Lovely," Sully said. "Still got Les to wake up yet. Might be dead for all we know."

Andy hoped not. The older man was part of the glue that held the team together. Well, except for Sully. That guy was a wildcard.

"He's not dead," Ben said.

"How the fuck do you know?" Sully spouted.

"He—Look, I don't know. Just don't give up on him."

"He's so old," Willie said in a deep, almost grunting voice.

Andy shook his head, grabbed three more rifles and slapped mags in them. There was no way he could carry extra ammo without fumbling something. He intended to bring guns to everyone, but that was nearly impossible now with Brent gone.

Four rifles were more than enough for him to haul.

He turned, still waiting for the suit to locate Ben and the others, when the helmet visor lit up in red words under the green.

NONHUMAN LIFEFORM APPROACHING.

Andy sucked in a sharp breath, glanced around and used the mild boost jets to hide behind the large rock again. He waited there, breath held, for over a minute. But nothing showed itself.

NONHUMAN LIFEFORM APPROACHING.

"Direction for nonhuman form," Andy tried.

Under the warning flashed: NW.

Northwest.

Along the very top and stretched along the visor was a compass. The green dot rested between west and south. Andy turned, watching the green dot skim over west. He stopped turning when the dot was between north and west. He stared down the main tunnel. The direction the massive creature disappeared.

Was it coming back?

Maybe it knew he was there?

Maybe it was returning to finish the job?

Gods, he didn't know and he decided not to stick around and find out.

"Locate human lifeforms," he told the suit.

A series of beeps and another green dot appeared just a hair above the compass. He turned until the dot was dead center and gaped at not the smaller tunnel, but another passageway a few feet to the right. He hadn't noticed it before because of the rock wall contours. The way they rose and fell. How they were so smooth to be both hypnotizing and mesmerizing. Even now, while he stared at the mouth of yet another small tunnel, Andy found himself adrift. He could see himself living down here.

He reached out a hand to feel the wall. All those reds and browns and yellows and—

Long, needle-like teeth flashed inches from his outstretched arm.

Andy sucked in a sharp breath and spun just in time to drop the other rifles and hold one up for protection. The toothy mouth clamped down on the gun, digging deep grooves and punctures into the plastic and metal. The mouth yanked the gun out of his grip, pulling it to the maw of...

"What the...hell?"

"What's going on?" Ben said through the helmet speakers.

The gun was too long to be sucked into the maw, so the mouth released it. The creature's head whipped from side to side, long snout nearly bashing into Andy before he moved away. Nothing as large as the creature that ate Brent, but not small either.

"Andy?"

"I don't know what this thing is," Andy said. "Medium boost." The suit's jets shot him backward to the large rock. "Stop boost."

"What's she look like?" Sully asked.

Andy peered around the rock. His eyes widened and his heart skipped a beat. "It's gone."

"What'ya mean she's gone?" Sully sounded like he was on the verge of tears, or something.

Andy floated back behind the rock, trying to calm his frantic heart.

"The fuck is goin' on?" Sully spouted.

"I don't know," Andy said, turning so his back rested against the rock. "I—"

The pink mouth filled with sharp teeth darted at his face, scratching the visor. He ducked, avoiding another slingshot snap from the mouth.

"*Shit*," he managed while scrambling away.

"Goddamn it," Les said. "The hell is goin' on, Andy? Report!"

"Oh," he said as he inched his way back toward the guns. "Ya know, just trying not to get eaten. Like one does."

"Funny," Ben said.

"I thought it was funny," Sully said and chuckled a bit.

"Shut up," Les said. "Both of you. Andy, you really need to let us know what's going on. What's trying to eat you?"

"How the hell am I supposed to know. Looks like a shark, but it's got a long nose and its mouth is weird."

"Shoots out like a slingshot, aye?" Sully asked.

"Yes," Andy said and added, "Low boost."

The suit propelled him to the floating guns. He snatched one up, swung around and—

The creature was gone. Again.

Andy, shivering, turned in a slow circle. But the creature was nowhere in sight. Well, as far as he could tell, anyway. The suit's lifeform tracker only picked up human lifeforms. He lowered the gun, gaze drifting back and forth.

After a few minutes, he gave in and checked the area.

Nothing.

The thing must have thought Andy too difficult and moved on. Wasted energy. Or it just got bored. Which, Andy supposed, was about the same thing.

A long sigh whispered out of him and he gathered the four guns he had dropped.

He turned back to the small tunnel where the rest of the team waited.

CHAPTER 15

The tunnel was about the same size as the other smaller one, though its walls were ragged and lacked any color whatsoever. Perhaps because there wasn't a current. Or if so, the flow was too minimal to erode the rock much.

About six feet in diameter, it was narrower than the other, but not so much to really get under Andy's skin. There was enough space around him where he didn't feel too constricted.

HUMAN LIFEFORMS – 6 METERS.

Andy blinked and slowed the suit's booster jets to low. He drifted down the tunnel, frowning. Six meters was only about nineteen feet. He should be able to see them. He should—

Something heavy slammed into his back, driving him to the jagged floor of the tunnel. The suit's proximity alarms blared. Andy grunted, tried rolling around to shoot whatever struck him but he was pinned.

DAMAGE REPORT: LIGHT, flashed red letters across the visor. DAMAGE INCREASING.

Whatever held him down was trying to tear him apart. He kicked, tried throwing an elbow or two, but nothing connected.

"Andy?" Ben asked. "You alright, man?"

"Something has me pinned," Andy said. "Taking damage."

"How far away are you?"

Andy grunted, trying to move, but it was no use. "Tell your suit to locate human lifeforms. I'm about six meters from you."

"I heard you saying that and didn't know if it was only you who could do that or…

"No. We all can."

DAMAGE INCREASING, flashed the red letters.

"Locate human lifeforms," Ben said.

"The hell we playin' hide'n'seek for?" Sully spouted. "How'd we get separated in the first place?"

Andy was flung to the side. He struck the ragged wall, but not hard enough to damage anything. He turned, lifting the gun, and hesitated.

It was the same creature that attacked him before. He was sure of it. Before he could pull the trigger, its mouth shot out and snapped inches from his face. Andy shifted, pointed the gun, and fired. The water filled with scarlet and bits of white flesh as the bullets sheared into the creature.

"Backward boost," he said, and the suit propelled him out of all the scarlet cloud.

Something moved within that cloud, but he couldn't pinpoint it enough to shoot. So, he waited. Eventually, the cloud would dissipate and reveal his target.

"Holy shit," Sully said. "The hell is that?"

"It's blood, you idiot," Les said.

"Hey," Sully said. "Listen here, ya'ol bastard. I'll—"

"Shut up," Ben said. "Both of you. We're here, Andy."

One of them drifted to his left side and shot a thumbs-up gesture. He wasn't sure who it was but gave a nod in return. Floating somewhere in the mess of blood were the other guns. It just needed to clear enough to see.

It burst out of the blood cloud and surged toward Andy. Its mouth shot out, snapped, retracted and just as it was about to slingshot out again, he shot it three times in the head. The first shot obliterated its long snout while the other two ruined that snapping mouth and destroyed an eye.

Still, it barreled at him.

"Quick burst, right," he said and the suit slammed him into the wall, narrowly avoiding the creature.

It left a bloody trail in its wake.

"Fuckin' hell," Sully muttered.

The suit still shoved Andy into the rocky wall. "Stop burst." The suit stopped and he swam around in time to see the creature, nose down, partially sunk on the tunnel's floor. Its long tail curled off and down from the ceiling.

Then the gentle current shifted and buried it in a cloud of blood.

The others moved around him. No one said anything for a minute or two.

It was Sully who broke it. "Goddamn goblin shark."

"A...goblin shark?" Ben asked.

"Aye. Goblin shark. Figured she'd be just that by Andy's description. Ugly bastards. Been around since the dinosaurs, so they say."

"What the hell is it doing in the tunnels?" Les asked.

"Hard t'say. Could be trapped like that old great white, or it's doing whatever the feck gobbies do."

"Gobbies?"

Sully sighed. "Do I really gotta explain this to ya, arsehole?"

Ben didn't reply.

"There's something else in these tunnels too," Andy said. "Huge. It swallowed Brent whole." Andy's eyes widened. "Shit. It did the same slingshot thing with its mouth like this one."

"No one really knows how large gobbies get, or very much 'bout 'em b'sides they were around way back in the dino days. Even that's sketchy to me, but, ya know…who am I, right?"

"But this thing," Andy said, "it was bigger than a great white."

"Sure t'was, boyo. Not denyin' ya a bit. The attacks on humans be rare, but then again, we don't get out'n'swim with them either. Too deep where they live."

"So," Les said. "There's a really big one swimming around yet? Does anyone know which direction we're supposed to go?"

"Wait," Andy said and faced the guys. "How'd you all get down here? There's little to no current, so it's not like you got sucked down here after the sub exploded."

"Maybe the blast threw us down here?" Eldon ventured.

"Were you all wrapped up in a ball so you'd go to the same place?" Andy asked.

No one replied to that.

Something was off and he didn't like it. "What the hell is going on?"

One of them drifted until he was directly in front of Andy. Through the visor, he noted Les's bearded face.

"Look," Les said, "we work for Wexler and were hired to take out Brent before the delivery and oust Guerra's operation."

Andy blinked. "So…you guys were never loyal to Brent?" He backed away a bit. Not because he was afraid, but he didn't like people too close to him. "Sully sure as hell played a good game, then."

"Up your arse, fecker."

"We all had our roles to play," Les said. "Except Willie. Poor kid was better left believing Brent was his boss. Would've got him all confused, otherwise."

Andy shook his head and glanced around. The blood cloud had dissipated enough to give him a full view of the goblin shark that tried to eat him. "Still doesn't answer how you all got in this tunnel."

"Made a pact," Ben said. "Whoever was conscious in the event of something happening to the sub, was supposed to get everyone away from Brent. Then, when we all gained consciousness, we would take him out."

"Fecker owed me two million for the last job," Sully interjected. "Hope he rots in Hell."

So, from what Andy was gathering, whoever was awake after the blast, had to pull each member of the team away from Brent. Why they picked the smallest tunnel and why he wasn't pulled along was still a mystery.

"Well," Andy said, "thanks for bringing me along, assholes."

The silence between them was palpable. He almost turned away to leave them to whatever demise they were aimed for, then stopped himself and faced Les.

"Spill it," Andy said. "All of it. No more games or role playing or whatever the hell you're all doing. I want the truth."

For the longest time, he wasn't sure if anyone would say anything. He began to turn away when Les said, "We're former Elite Patrol officers who work for Angela Wexler to stop the black water runners and their drug lords, like Guerra. That's what the Black Water Project really is. It's us and a couple of other teams. Brent was our mark for years and he finally trusted us enough to take us along on a run like this."

"So," Andy said, "all the stuff about not trusting Sully or Willie, or even Eldon, was all bullshit?"

"Wait a tick," Sully spouted. "You don't trust *me*? I mean, fine, but leave Eldon alone. Aye. Poor kid can't even tie his shoes without cutting himself on something."

"Whatever," Eldon said, not sounding the least amused.

Les ignored Sully and said, "Yeah. I had to."

"The hell?" Andy said. "All that did was make me paranoid and now totally confused."

"Sorry about that," Les said. "We needed to keep you on your toes while trying to highlight how bad Brent was. He was playing you too. Trying to turn you against me. Remember that stupid story he told you about me killing all those kids? Yup. He was working on you. And when the time came, he'd have you put a bullet in my head."

Even though Andy shook his head, Les was right. Brent was a persuasive and manipulative bastard. Andy wasn't so sure he'd get talked into killing someone, but...

"So," Andy said, "you all were in on it?"

"All but Willie," Ben said.

"What?" Willie said. "Who's talking? Hello? It smells weird in here."

Sully snorted and said, "Welp, the big bugger is awake now."

"Where are you guys?"

Andy couldn't help but smile. "You guys just left him?"

"Yeah, well, we figured we'd try to help you, so..." Ben said.

"Right."

"Guys? *Guys*? Ah, God. Am I dead? This Hell? I hear everyone talking but—"

"We're on our way, big guy," Ben said. "Settle down."

"Who was that?"

Ben sighed. "It's Ben. We're on our way. Don't move."

"Oh," Willie said. "Okay."

"Also," Sully said and pointed at the dead goblin shark, "if there's more sharks in this tunnel system, we should probably get away from this thing. The blood'll attract more."

The four snatched up their submersible assault rifles and banded around Andy.

"Okay," Andy said. "Let's get Willie and figure out how to get out of this in one piece."

As they used their boosters to move down the tunnel, Sully spouted, "Lookit that. Brent's not even dead for an hour'n'the guy already thinks he's the boss."

"I hope not," Andy said. "I have no goddamn idea what I'm doing."

Someone chuckled. Maybe Les.

Ben said, "Neither do we. At this point, whoever can get us the fuck outta here will be my boss. Until then, whoever comes up with the best ideas will be boss. Something like that."

"Uh-huh," Sully said. "How'd ya feel 'bout that poor shark back there? Bet ya were itchin' to bury'er, aye?" An obvious play on Ben's affection for animals.

"Shut up, Sully."

"Ah, hell," the Irishman said. "Struck a nerve."

"No," Ben said. "You're just a fuckin' idiot."

"Hey! Eldon resembles that remark!"

A single sigh floated through the speakers. Andy assumed it to be Eldon. Probably, it was.

And, thankfully, everyone fell silent until they reached a small cave at the end of the tunnel where Willie waited.

Then all hell broke loose.

CHAPTER 16

Andy wasn't sure who, but one of the men drifted in front of Willie.

Several streams of tiny bubbles appeared. All of them shot at the man in front of Willie and the man was consumed in bubbles.

Andy boosted away.

"Ah, shit," Sully said. "The bastard's found us."

Andy spun, spotted three in suits like his, boosting toward him. He lifted the rifle and squeezed off a couple of rounds, striking one of them through the visor of the helmet. An explosion of bubbles consumed the person and sent the other tumbling off to the side.

"Light 'em up," Ben said.

The two remaining soon went up in an explosion of bubbles.

"Ah, God," Willie groaned.

Andy turned to find the man in the burst suit. Rivers of red squiggled out of a split abdomen and clouded the water around him. A loop of blue-gray intestines poked out of the tear in the man's abdomen. Only thing that remained intact was the helmet. Andy squinted at the gaping face through the visor and spun away before he vomited. Which, in the suit, wouldn't be good at all.

He drifted away, gagging while the others moved in Willie's direction.

Silence stole over the team.

Andy looked away from the tattered, bobbing dead bodies of their attackers and stared at a ragged wall. He closed his eyes, trying to calm his stomach. If he vomited, he'd die. Then his kids wouldn't have anyone. He needed to stay alive for them. They were what mattered most. Even if he wasn't getting the money promised, escaping this fuckery alive and seeing his children again was paramount.

"Ah, hell," Ben said.

"Shit," Sully said.

The urge to vomit subsided a bit and Andy managed, "What?"

A stretch of silence greeted him.

"Poor ol' bastard," Sully said after what felt like hours.

Andy blinked, the greasy feeling in his stomach melted away, replaced by a piercing chill which doubled him over a bit. "Les?" he said.

"Aye," Sully said. "He saved ol' Willie."

Les was like the glue that held the team together. The foundation to keep them from sinking. He was smart and cared about people. Something, though he tried, Brent never was. It also proved what kind of man he was.

He threw himself into the line of fire to save Willie. He was a hero, in that regard, at least.

Andy turned and looked at the floating corpse. The suit was a tattered mess, having burst open from groin to collarbone. Likewise, the man's torso. A ruination of flesh and shattered bone from all the pressure.

He lowered his head and sighed. A tear trickled down his cheek.

"He has a wife," Ben said. "We should bring him with us for her."

"He does?" Eldon asked. "I didn't know that."

"He tried to leave family at the door when he came to work. I wouldn't have known if we hadn't been trapped in that pillbox in Afghanistan for two days. We got on the subject of families and, well, he let slip he was married."

"The blood'll make us direct targets to any predators down here," Sully said, not a touch of emotion in his tone. "Best to leave'im and get the hell outta here."

"Sully is right," Andy said. "We need to get away from here before something else comes."

"The current is almost nonexistent," Sully said. "But it's here. Water flows into this tributary, finds the dead end and flows back out." He nodded toward the mouth of the tunnel. "Once it flows out, all the blood will go with it to the main tunnel. We best haul arse."

"Let's move," Andy said, not caring anymore who they wanted to be their new leader. Sully was most definitely right. Time to go.

***

They left Les there at the end of the dead-end tunnel. A man Andy barely knew, but liked, regardless. A man he could see being good friends with down the road.

A man who sacrificed himself to save another.

A true soldier.

A hero.

The blood beat them out of the tunnel, regardless of the slow current.

"Which way?" Ben asked, mostly to himself.

They floated near the large rock Brent had emerged around in what felt like ages ago now. The current tugged Andy toward the direction where the giant creature disappeared. His gaze lifted to the massive hole they created to enter the ancient tunnel in the first place. If they went up there, how many more of Guerra's men would be waiting and how many would eventually hunt them down?

He turned around very slowly, keeping an eye on the stretched compass across his helmet's visor. They needed to go north. Didn't matter where they came ashore anymore, as long as they made it to land. The next step would be contacting Wexler.

But, one step at a time.

North ended up being the exact same direction the monstrous creature went. For all he knew, it was, indeed, a giant goblin shark, but his brain couldn't quite wrap around that idea. It was just too damn big. No matter what Sully said, the creature just couldn't be an overgrown goblin shark.

Andy pointed down the tunnel. "We have to go that way."

"Or," Sully said, "we can go up. Might have a run in with more of Guerra's assholes, but at least we'd be less likely to encounter somethin' else."

"They'd be in minisubs," Andy said. "We wouldn't stand a chance."

Sully didn't rebut the fact and fell silent again.

"So," Andy said, "our only real option is north, which is down the main tunnel here."

No one said anything.

He sighed and said, "Let's go." A few seconds later he boosted away from them, propelled down the main tunnel.

If they followed, he didn't know, nor did he check.

This was it.

Regardless if they followed or not…this was it.

CHAPTER 17

They did though.

Didn't take long before Ben and Eldon were gliding on either side of him while he drifted down the tunnel. Well, more than drifting, his visor informed him he was cruising at a nice sixty miles per hour. He didn't stop to take in the scenery or check the darker areas as he continued onward. The other two, Sully and Willie, didn't trail far behind.

Despite everything, Andy felt Sully had been close to Brent. Or, at the very least, reasonably close. The guy wasn't ready to follow a new leader yet. Especially one that wouldn't pay out anything except, maybe, saving his life.

Andy just hoped the Irishman wouldn't go crazy and try to kill him or someone else.

He'd need to keep an eye on Sully and Willie for a while.

"Ben," Andy said. "Eldon. Get your lifeform locators on."

"Ten-four," Ben said.

"Just tell the suit, right?" Eldon asked.

"Yep."

Both men ordered the suit to locate lifeforms. Andy followed suit. The visor read: 0 NON-HUMAN LIFEFORMS. He blew out a breath too heavy to be a sigh and tried to relax a little. Whatever that massive creature was, maybe it was long gone now. Or so far ahead the suit's locator couldn't ping it. Which was fine too.

Ahead, the main tunnel broke off in a lazy four-way intersection. More meandering than straight and perfect crossroads. The tunnels on the left and right snaked away while the main tunnel continued north.

"Stay in the main tunnel," Andy said. "We're heading in the right direction."

No one responded, nor did he expect them to. If they followed, they followed. If not…it was their choice. He needed to get to his kids. They were the most important thing. They were always the most important.

After a few minutes, Sully said, "How far are we away from the coast?"

"Last I remember," Eldon said, "we're three hundred miles from the coast of Texas."

"Well, hell, we weren't as far into this thing as I thought."

"Not even halfway," Eldon said.

"I think we should—holy fuck! Look out!"

It came out of the deeper shadows. Not necessarily moving fast, but as the team boosted over sixty miles per hour, it seemed like the damn thing was a torpedo.

It bashed into Eldon, flung him aside and barreled into Andy. His entire world became a tumbling series of chaos and when it all stopped, he was aware of only two things. The boosters stopped, and he was going to puke. He swallowed down the hot spit flooding his mouth and clamped his eyes shut from the motion sickness trying to take over. Like that time when he was twelve and his friends pressured him onto The Spider. A ride at the county fair he managed to avoid until that fateful evening with his friends.

At first, it wasn't so bad, but then the kid sharing the slick, black car they rode in bellowed, "Spinner!" The kid was Max Wright. All two hundred pounds of him. He outweighed Andy by at least one hundred pounds and swung the car around faster than it would have normally done. No matter how much Andy cried for Max to stop, the kid either didn't hear or care. The spinning continued. Howling laughter filled his ears. The massive weight of Max practically crushed him with every other turn.

Andy screamed for the ride to stop. He cried for it to all stop.

But the ride didn't stop.

Somehow, he managed to make it through to the end. Just outside the gate, though, he hit his knees and vomited into the grass.

All the tumbling now, it felt like that long-ago evening on The Spider. A sense of hopelessness. The realization the world might very well end. The spinning and tilting were so severe, he just closed his eyes and waited for death.

And yet, like The Spider, his insides seemed to spin while the outside stopped. He pinched his eyes shut, swallowing down gags and forcing himself not to acknowledge the proverbial greasy ball slipping in his stomach.

Somewhere within the spinning stew, Ben said, "Shoot it!"

Andy swallowed down a thick lump in his throat and, eventually, the internal spinning stopped. He let out a burp, which made the helmet reek for a few, long seconds, then opened his eyes.

The scene before him was a stormy blood cloud. Every now and then a dark shadow moved within the cloud. Like something—

It burst out of the cloud, mouth full of needle-like teeth snapping at him. They missed by a good inch or two. He swam backwards to avoid the large shark.

Yes. A shark. Just like the last one. Only, perhaps, a bit larger.

"Can't see shit with all the blood," Sully said. "She dead?"

"I don't know," Ben said. "Andy, you okay?"

He cleared his throat, keeping an eye on the big goblin shark. It bumped into the wall, like it didn't know how to swim anymore. Andy quickly saw why. One of its pectoral fins was badly damaged and there were a few holes seeping thick tendrils of blood near its head. Its mouth shot out every couple of seconds, or so. Then the shark was hidden with a new cloud of blood.

"Andy?"

"Here," he said and swam away from the injured creature. "Coming your way. Don't shoot me."

"Aw, man," Sully spouted. "There goes m'day."

Andy emerged from the blood cloud and stopped. All four men pointed their guns at him. His heart stuttered. "I said don't shoot me."

They lowered their guns and he blew out a sigh of relief. He swam the rest of the way to them. The boosters just felt unnecessary being so close.

"You alright?" Ben asked.

"Yeah. Just got tossed around a bit too much. It's hurt bad through all that blood. Confused and bumping into the wall."

"Need to put her outta'er misery," Sully said.

"Too dangerous," Andy said. "It'll die eventually."

"Pretty cruel thing to say," Ben said.

"Aye," Sully said.

Once he found Ben, Andy frowned at him through the visor. "We're sitting ducks here with all the blood. Blood was we were trying to hurry away from, remember?"

But it was Sully who responded. "I might be a bastard, but I'm not a feckin' bastard. We need to end its misery, boyo."

He was right, but Andy worried about all the blood. There was just so much...

"We have time," Sully added.

"Okay," Andy said. "Let's make it quick."

No one said anything and they all plunged through the blood cloud to find the poor goblin shark still bumping along the wall. The blood cleared enough to see it from time to time. Ben and Sully were right. It needed to be mercifully dispatched. A fact Andy knew, though figured getting away from it all would be safer.

Nobody moved, so Andy placed the muzzle of his rifle on top of the shark's head and pulled the trigger. Four rounds blasted the creature before Andy let up and swam backward. More blood clouded the water. But one thing was for sure, the shark was dead. It sank slowly to the floor of the tunnel even before the blood obscured it.

The others floated and stared at him.

"Let's go." He swam by and said, "Mild boost."

The suit's thrusters engaged and propelled him away from the team and the carnage.

He kept a wary eye on the shadows and ignored Ben when he called for Andy to wait for them.

A stupid thing to do, he supposed, but he needed to get away from them for a few seconds. He needed to think. It wasn't about ending a shark's misery, but how they ganged up on him. How Sully appeared to be in charge for a second or two.

Does it really matter who's in charge?

Andy shook his head, trying to keep an eye out for any more sharks. No, it didn't matter much. Except, he still didn't fully trust Sully yet.

"Low boost," he said and sighed. When the suit slowed to a drift, he said, "Stop."

The current still pushed him along, but at least he wasn't going sixty miles per hour anymore.

"I see the fecker now," Sully said. "Eh! Arsehat! Ya forgot us."

When the others gathered around him, Andy said, "We need to get out of this tunnel."

"Aye," Sully said. "The blood."

The Irishman didn't sound pushy, just agreeable. Which threw Andy some.

He shook it off and glanced around. "We should've taken one of the other tunnels at the intersection."

"You told us to go straight," Eldon said.

"I know." He frowned and stared straight ahead. "I was trying to get us out of here the quickest why I could. I was wrong. The main tunnel is like bleeding and swimming through a tube with hidden piranha."

"Well," Ben said, "that's definitely accurate so far."

"Piranha?" Willie spouted. "We gotta fight them *too*?"

"Settle down, ya stupid oaf," Sully said.

It took Willie a full five seconds. "Hey! That's not nice!"

Everyone, including Andy, chuckled.

"So," Ben said after a minute or so. "What are we going to do?"

Andy, drifting with the current down the main tunnel, shrugged. "We find the right tunnel."

Everyone fell silent.

Ahead lay only darkness.

CHAPTER 18

The tunnel didn't branch off, though. Instead, it meandered on. Every so often there would come a gentle turn, but other than that, there weren't even any tributaries. No small tunnels. Just the mesmerizing walls, ceiling and floor of the main tunnel. All that smooth, colorful, flowing stone.

Andy forced himself not to look at it for too long. He focused on the tunnel ahead. The lifeforms alert read: 0. But that didn't seem to matter because the last goblin shark about took him out without any warning at all. Not even a beep from the suit. So, it wasn't like he could trust it much. Maybe a little, but not enough to save his or the others' lives. Vigilance was key. Keep their eyes peeled and senses sharp.

A thought surfaced in his mind. "That's two confirmed goblin sharks in the same tunnel. Does that happen often?"

No one responded right away. He listened to himself and the other men breathe for what felt like hours.

Finally, Sully said, "I dunno. Could be just lost down here."

Andy frowned. "Spawning, maybe? Like fish?"

"Like fi—the hell ya goin' on 'bout? No, not like fish. Goblin sharks, like most of 'em, have internal fertilization."

"What's internal festerization?" Willie asked.

"I—Yeah, I can't even with you right now, ya oaf. Internal *fertilization*. Means they gotta—"

"Fuck," Ben said.

"Bingo, boyo," Sully said.

Andy's gaze drifted back and forth. He wished the helmet's visor would clear things up further than fifty yards. Anything could be lurking in the deep shadows. Watching…waiting…

"So," he said, hoping Sully was paying attention, "what if these tunnels are their mating grounds?"

A tick of silence, then, "There'd be more of 'em, though. Least, I'd think so. Bloody mess, mating sharks. Watched some nursies—"

"What?" Ben said.

Sully sighed. "Nursies. Nurse sharks, f'shit sake."

"Oh."

"Anyway. Nice shallow waters and there they be, just goin' at it. Bitin'n' thrashin' about. The water's all pink like there's some kinda massacre goin' on below the surface."

"But it's possible they were in here to mate," Andy said, drawing Sully back to the real issue.

"Aye. Possible. Not likely, but possible."

Andy nodded. "Maybe they were trying to find their way out." He paused, then added, "I just don't know what that really big creature is, for sure."

"The tunnel is like a damn ongoin' cavern. Could be a whale of some sort."

"No," Andy said. "This thing had teeth like the goblin sharks, just way larger."

Sully grunted. "Aye. Ya said this. But ya might be mistaken too. All happened so fast, ya know."

Andy glared straight ahead. "I saw what I saw."

"And I'm not disputin' that. Just sayin', could be somethin' else. Far as I know, gobbies don't grow that big. Fifteen to twenty feet be pushin' it. Like those feckers that attacked us."

"Right," Andy said, drifting into thought.

Les. If Les was here, he would know what to do. Or, at least, have a better idea than Andy. Tears welled in Andy's eyes. They hadn't been close, but there was a friendship brewing. The older man didn't deserve what happened. Should've just let the bastards turn Willie into Swiss cheese. *That's mean*, Andy thought. *Willie isn't bright, but that doesn't mean you have to wish death on him.*

The big guy was docile enough. Just a simple person following whatever orders were given to him. Not his fault, really.

Still, there was some resentment. Why take Les? Why?

Andy glowered at the shadows. In every spot of darkness, he saw the long snouted head of a goblin shark. He saw its darting mouth. But the way it bit down on over half of Brent's body…

It begged the question, though: What the hell was it?

If too big to be a goblin shark, then what ate Brent? A feat only a very large great white could accomplish since Brent was so tall. Maybe even a huge tiger shark.

But it wasn't a great white.

It wasn't a tiger shark.

For now, Andy chalked it up as a monster and nothing more. Because it was. Heart thrumming, he focused on the tunnel. The dark shadows and whorls cut into the flowing walls. The—

A silver stream whizzed by and a small section of the rock wall to the right exploded, creating a tiny gray cloud.

His stomach lurched. "Behind us! Stop boosters."

The suit's thrusters quit and he wished he hadn't said anything at all. The full stop jarred him so badly, all the air whooshed out of his lungs like someone gut punched him. He gasped for air and couldn't find it for a few ungodly seconds.

The others at least had the good sense to allow their suits to slow down first.

Through his helmet, the team shouted.

"Bastards just won't stop," Ben said.

"Got one," Willie said.

"Feckers," Sully said. "This is for Les!"

Eldon didn't shout or say anything at all.

Once Andy could breathe again, he turned to find the fight all but over. Ben held one of Guerra's men in a bear hug.

"The hell ya doin'?" Sully asked.

"Going to tell him to tell his crew, or whoever, to stop pursuing us or they'll all die."

Andy almost chuckled. Almost. "Um. He can't hear you." He swam up next to Ben.

Ben glanced at Andy. "He—ah, shit. Duh."

"And they say Willie is the dumb one," Sully muttered.

"Wait, what?" Willie said.

"Well, o'course I said, 'And they say Willie is the awesome one.'"

"Oh. Okay."

Sully snorted.

Ben let Guerra's man go and Eldon shot him in the head. A burst of scarlet bubbles consumed the man's head, then he floated, face down.

'Holy shit," Sully spouted. "Little warnin' next time."

"Sorry," Eldon said.

Andy frowned at the guy, not sure what to say. Eldon lowered his gun and tuned to face Andy. They locked gazes for a second or more, then Eldon moved away. Andy watched him drift by Sully. He continued away from the group a few yards, stopped swimming, floated for a bit and turned back to the team.

"I need to tell you guys something," Eldon said.

"What?" Andy said, while he and the others swam closer to Eldon.

"Wexler knows about the sharks."

Andy stopped swimming. "What do you mean she knows?"

Eldon lowered his head a bit. "I've worked for Wexler longer than I worked for Brent. Longer than my military career."

"Ya fuckin' piss hat," Sully said, voice low and guttural. "You been playin' us the whole time? We're pals, you'n'I."

"Yes, we're friends. But, listen, Wexler isn't the bad guy. She wants a blood sample from the largest shark we can find down here. She believes it might help the Black Water research team in discovering a cure for AIDS. I believe it too."

"How does she know the goblin sharks are here and how does she know their blood might help in a cure?" Andy asked, honestly curious.

"We're in the black water right now, fecker," Sully said.

Eldon appeared to ignore the Irishman. "It was a fluke, really." He pointed up the tunnel. "Sometime in the last couple of years, a large goblin shark was tagged while Wexler was developing her facility. Her own team tagged it. A month ago, the tag pinged at these coordinates."

"Okay," Andy said, frowning at Eldon. "So, how did Brent know to enter this lower system?"

"He didn't. I told him about it before we deployed. I gave him a rudimentary layout map of the tunnels and pinpointed where we needed to go to enter this older system. All he knew was what I showed him."

Everyone fell silent for a moment or two.

"I gotta pee," Willie said.

Sully made a huge, dramatic sigh. "Goddamn it, ya oaf. I told ya t'go before we left!"

The big man's voice quivered a bit. "Sorry. I just...can I get out of the suit to pee?"

"*No*," Andy said, heart trip-hammering. "You open the suit and you'll be crushed to death. Go in the suit, if you have to. Just do *not* open the suit while we're in the tunnels, okay?"

A pause. "Okay."

"That's gonna stink," Ben said.

"Better than being dead," Andy said.

"Touché."

Andy returned his attention to Eldon. "So, we're supposed to hunt down the largest goblin shark here and take a blood sample? Like it's all some stroll through the park?"

"Well," Eldon said, "I do have a special long-range extraction gun. Effective up to fifty feet."

Andy nodded. "That might work if—"

The jaws snapped horizontally around most of Eldon's torso. They pinned his arms to his sides and clamped him tight. Tendrils of scarlet bubbles flowed from between the long teeth embedded into Eldon.

"Oh *shit*," Sully spouted.

Eldon gurgled, though managed, "Ex...traction...gun. Hip."

Andy glanced at Eldon's hips and blinked. He hadn't noticed the small gun fixed to the utility belt. Without thinking, he swam forward and took hold of the extraction gun. A contraption no larger than a potbelly forty-five revolver. Stuck in the small barrel was what appeared to be a thick needle. He went to detach the gun from the belt when suddenly he was being yanked forward with Eldon. The mouth was sucking them into its gullet. It was about to eat them both.

He pulled on the blood extraction gun, though to no avail, and reached for the clasp holding it to Eldon's belt.

Darkness crowded around as the mouth dragged him closer toward the creature's gullet. He sucked in a sharp breath, pressed the clasp and swam away, gripping the blood extraction gun a millisecond before the mouth opened for a wider bite.

"Holy hell," Sully shouted. "Swim, ya American bastard! It's right there!"

Andy, barely breathing, kicked and stroked with everything he had away from the massive shark. Still not as large at the one that ate Brent, but big enough. Yes. Big enough for sure.

"*Go*," Ben said. "Jesus, *go!*"

For the life of him, Andy couldn't tell the suit to use the boost thrusters. Every time he tried, all that fell out were a few squeaks. Fear choked him. He swam until he ran into one of the other guys. Only then did he calm down enough to stop. He turned in time to watch Eldon be yanked into the maw and consumed. His death was silent, though struck a hard nerve.

Another one of the team was gone. The only person who might have had an idea of what the hell was happening just got eaten. Eldon was always stand-offish, and now Andy knew exactly why. He was dedicated to Wexler, rather than Brent or the money. Even Ben or Les followed the money instead of full loyalty. Sully only really cared about money, or so it seemed. And Willie…well, Willie cared about making everyone happy. Even if the one he was making happy was the villain. To Willie, it didn't matter. All depended on how people treated and coerced him to one side or another. The guy knew better, but Andy felt true realization didn't happen until a few minutes after the fact. Or if at all. The man was slow, though not exactly stupid.

"Keep firing," Ben said.

"Spread out," Sully shouted. "Fecker's not slowin' down."

Andy faced the goblin shark and realized he was the only one still in the monster's path. Blood turned the water scarlet as it bared down on him. He sucked in a breath, lifted his gun and—

Something struck him hard on the right, shoving him to the left with so much force he struggled not to tumble. He spun, ready to blast anything and everything apart with his rifle.

The giant stature of the man in front of him was unmistakable.

"Willie?"

The big man turned to look at Andy and smiled a second before the shark's jaws shot out and snagged him. He struggled. Andy's helmet filled with grunts and curses. But Willie fought the beast. He roared, trying to pry the long teeth out of him. Even if he managed to break free, the teeth turned him into Swiss cheese. Bloody bubbles frothed and streamed from around the teeth.

Andy pointed his gun at the huge goblin shark and squeezed the trigger. Several rounds plunged into the creature's head, though it never released Willie. Eventually, the monster sagged and sank to the tunnel's floor with Willie still trapped in its jaws.

"Ah, hell," Sully muttered.

"G-Guys," Willie said. "I…I don't feel good."

Everyone, even Sully, swam to the big man still clutched in those long, needle-like teeth.

"Shh," Andy said, lowering himself beside the man. They were never close, but then again, who was Willie close to anyway?

Everyone just saw him as a tool. Something they could use. They never thought of Willie as a person who had feelings. Even Andy. The man never really had any friends and Andy placed a hand on the visor of the helmet.

"I'm so sorry," he told the big man, tears welling in his eyes. Perhaps the very tears repressed from Les's death. Or, maybe, all the deaths combined so far. Deaths that shouldn't have happened.

"A-Andy," Willie said. "I…I…"

"Shh," Andy said. "It's okay."

"No," Willie managed after a few labored breaths. "B…Be…"

"You'll be alright," Sully said, interrupting the big man. "We're all here, lad."

Sully, it turned out, continued to surprise Andy. The guy never appeared overly emotional or super involved with anything. But the few times he'd shown something akin to caring, it all appeared genuine.

"B…B…" Willie said, voice turning to gurgles.

"What?" Andy said. He moved closer, as if Willie could whisper him a secret.

"B…Be…t-tri-trick…" A long sigh blew through the speaker of Andy's helmet.

Willie's body slackened. His head lowered. It was like watching a balloon slowly deflate.

Andy shook him. "Willie?"

The big man didn't move, nor did he respond.

Andy backed away.

"Wonder what the oaf was tryin't'say?" Sully said. "Somethin' 'bout a trick, aye?"

"I don't know," Andy said, frowning at the dead man. His gaze stretched to the large goblin shark before returning to Willie. "Sounded important."

"We should get moving, guys," Ben said.

Andy nodded. "Yeah."

"Lot'o blood now," Sully said. "If there be more down here, they'll find us."

"Let's move, then," Andy said. He swam away. "Stick close to the wall. Maybe we'll find another tunnel."

Ben collected the magazine from Willie's rifle.

Silence fell and Andy told the suit to mild boost.

They cruised close to the right wall. Each man had their lifeform locators on. Each man, Andy hoped, was keeping a close eye on the shadows ahead and the bleakness on the other side of the tunnel. A span of, Andy guessed, about eighty feet.

Ahead lay only darkness…

CHAPTER 19

"Ya know," Sully said, scooting to Andy's left side, "I didn't like you."

Andy snorted. "Didn't like you much either."

"Nah," Sully said. "Mine was worse. I wanted t'kill ya. Thought ya were a narc."

Andy glanced at Sully, though the Irishman's head was turned away.

"But ya proved me wrong. Haven't known ya more than a few days'n'ya outshined even ol' Benny back there."

"Hey," Ben spouted.

Andy smiled. "Well, thanks. I guess."

A beat of silence, then Sully said, "Ya gotta understand our code, boyo. Newcomers came before and proved to be infiltrators sent from other companies or squads. We're all guarded. Our operations are always covert. Taking in a new one, be it Elite or nah, we got problems from the get go."

"Understandable," Andy said, though he was not sure where Sully was going with all this.

"Gotta be trust, boyo. Gotta be. Aye. If there be no trust, the entire team eats itself." A slight pause. "Right, Benny?"

"Yup," Ben said.

The tunnel curved to the left. Not the direction Andy wanted but no other tunnels branched off the main one. They were trapped in a stone tube thousands of feet below the Gulf of Mexico. *Like cattle to the slaughter*, Andy thought.

A long stretch of time, a little over an hour according to the suit's clock, gave way to nothing but silence between the three men. Long enough for Andy's mind to wander a bit and his concentration on the tunnel to waver.

He cast the idea of the tunnels being breeding grounds aside for a moment. Why else would the goblin sharks be there? No food to speak of. Andy hadn't spotted a single stray fish. Confinement. They were limited in every way. As far as he knew, sharks couldn't swim backward. Say, if one were to grab a tail and pull a shark backward, it'd die. So, no backing up. They were forced to swim forward, even if it meant a dead-end. Unless they could turn around, they died. And, perhaps why they attacked so aggressively might mean they're starving and can't help it.

Or, Andy thought, *they're protecting something. Like guards protect a king or queen.*

It didn't make much sense, but the thought dug its claws in deep anyway.

What if they had sentries to protect something? Could sharks do that? Could they reason and plan?

He opened his mouth to ask Sully what he thought when the visor of his helmet blinked red and read: 2 NON-HUMAN LIFEFORMS.

"Slow boosters," Andy said.

The other two followed suit.

"Two non-human lifeforms," Ben said.

"Yeah," Sully spouted. "Got it."

"Keep to the wall," Andy said without thinking. Instincts took over. "Boosters stop." He said and sprawled against the smooth wall. "Stay flat. Let's see what's coming."

Neither Ben nor Sully said anything.

Andy frowned at the darkness beyond the visor's reach. A darkness so still, it might as well be a black wall. He lifted the submersible assault rifle and waited.

A stretch of time went by.

"Where are they?" Ben asked.

"Maybe these helmets are messin' up," Sully said.

Andy frowned at the wall of darkness. Maybe Sully was right. Maybe the helmets were glitching because there was nothing in the tunnel but them.

He sighed, lowered the gun and was about to turn to the guys when Sully said, "Oh, *shit*."

Andy spun back around and all the strength drained out of him. He couldn't lift the rifle even if he wanted to. His heart gave several quick bangs. A chill scuttled through him.

The thing was massive. Perhaps larger than the one that ate Brent. Long, pointy teeth protruded from its slightly open mouth. From pectoral fin to pectoral fin, Andy judged it was at least twenty feet wide, if not more. How long…well, that was yet to be seen. Its dark eyes revealed nothing. Just a bleak and vast emptiness from which there would be no return.

"Jesus," Sully said. "She's a big bastard."

The huge goblin shark swam on with slow, rhythmic movements of its tail. If it saw the men it gave no sign.

"Bigger than the one that ate Brent," Andy said.

"No shit?"

"No shit."

It took over five minutes for the creature to swim through.

"Gotta be 'bout forty feet long," Sully said.

"More like fifty," Ben said, voice weak.

Sully drifted away from the wall a bit and Andy pulled him back.

"What—"

"There's another one, remember?"

Sully, face expressionless through the visor, moved back to the wall.

"It's not right," Ben said. "They shouldn't be that big."

"What's ta'stop'em?" Sully spouted. "They've lived fer millions of years. That's millions of years of evolution. Once the big predators stopped going so deep, what's ta'stop the gobbies from just growin'n'growin'?" He shook his head. "They're the apex predators of the deep now."

Andy stared into the darkness, Sully's words reverberating through his head in mindless echoes. Was it really evolution, or something else? After the dinosaurs, everything seemed to shrink in size, adapting to the lessening oceans as Earth and life moved on. No one, even Sully, knew for sure what happened. It was all speculation.

The visor, despite showing two lifeforms, stopped blinking red around the edges and said: 0 NON-HUMAN LIFEFORMS.

"Damn thing counted as two," Ben said.

Still, Andy had them wait a few minutes longer. Just in case. But when nothing showed up, they swam away from the wall a bit.

"We should keep moving," Ben said after a few minutes.

Andy turned to the man. "I think we need to figure out a different route. Retrace and go back the tunnel system above this one. These tunnels are for the sharks."

Ben made a grunting sound. "Yeah, okay. We go up there and Guerra's men will blow us to shreds. This is our only option."

"Maybe they moved on," Sully said. "Maybe they think we're dead."

Ben chuckled humorously. "Yeah. Sure. You go first."

A spate of silence, then Sully said, "Well, aren't we actin' a bit outta character..."

Ben didn't respond.

Andy looked at Ben, but the guy only shrugged.

"Why aren't you at least willing to look?" Andy asked. "There's been a lot of blood. They might think we're dead."

Without pause, Ben said, "They know we're still alive." A long breath filled the speakers, then, "Shit."

"What the *actual* fuck, man?" Sully said.

Andy drifted away from Ben, eyes wide. "How do you know that?"

Ben sighed. "Alright, look. I work directly with Guerra. I'm his hitman, I guess you can say. I was to keep an eye on Brent and on this mission, take him out. Brent had become a liability."

"So," Andy said, "that's how you know we can't go back. They're either listening in or are tracking you."

"Both," Ben said. "I'm on their hitlist now. Hope you're both happy."

"You fuckin' bastard," Sully said and pointed his gun at Ben. "First El and his secret and now we find out you're workin' for a drug lord? Thought ya were a nice Iowa boy."

"I am," Ben said. "I just happen to work for Guerra. Well, used to. All bets are off now."

"Oh, boo-feckin'-hoo," Sully said. "Think Andy and I should fill ya with holes and be done with ya."

Ben held up his arms. "Might as well. Once we get out of here, he'll kill us all anyway."

Sully lowered the rifle. "We'll see. Aye, we'll see."

"Can you end communications with him?" Andy said, keeping his rifle ready. Just in case.

"No. I'd have to take off my helmet and rip the mic out."

"I vote he should do just that," Sully spouted.

Andy sighed. "Give me your gun."

"Why? I'm not going to shoot you guys."

"Says the goddamn *assassin*," Sully said.

A few ticks of silence, then Andy held his hand out to Ben. "The gun."

"What if you need help with the sharks?"

Andy chose not to answer and kept his hand held out for the gun. He lifted his own rifle to show Ben he was serious.

"Fine," Ben said and placed the gun in Andy's hand. "There. Feel better now?"

Andy slung it over a shoulder and nodded. "We'll see." He glanced at Sully. The Irishman still had his gun pointed at Ben. "Okay. Let's keep moving."

He wasn't used to being a leader, though knew he needed to be. At least for now. Even if he had no clue what he was doing. Sully was too emotional.

Andy motioned for Ben to go ahead of them. Ben appeared to understand and swam out in front. Even if Ben wouldn't really kill them, Andy wasn't going to take any chances. He needed this to all end. He needed to get back to his kids. He doubted he'd have a job at the border anymore, but maybe he could try his hand at being a fireman. Maybe.

He handed Ben's gun to Sully. "Low boosters. Let's go slow so the suits pick lifeforms up better." He hoped that was why the suits were sometimes late to the game. If not, it was a glitch of some sort. At least, that's what he assumed.

Better safe than sorry.

Slow it down, keep a better eye on everything. Let the suit do its scans. Perhaps dodge the sharks, rather than kill them.

Maybe that's all they needed to do to get out of this. Just keep it slow and steady. Avoid any danger when possible. Keep moving.

Yes, but unfortunately, nothing ever went as planned.

CHAPTER 20

"Feckin' hell," Sully shouted.

Andy spun, telling the suit to stop the boosters, vaguely aware of Ben doing the same because it took him a few seconds to fully grasp the scene before him.

The mouth covering most of Sully's upper half wasn't massive, but enough to send an icy chill through Andy. The bite radius was about the size of a very large great white. About twenty inches. As far as deep—

"I'm not supposed to see gills from the *inside*," Sully said. "The hell are ya feckers doin'? Lil'help here."

"Hold on," Andy said. "It's not moving."

"Oh, well, ain't that just peaches," Sully mumbled.

Andy swam to the side and gasped.

"No hurry at all," Sully spouted. "Not like I got a feckin' shark on my head, or anything."

"Jesus," Ben said.

"What?" Sully said.

Andy blew out a breath, drew in another and said, "Something bit in half."

A pause, then Sully said. "So…I got a dead, half eaten gobbie on my head?"

"Yeah."

"Lovely. I knew I shoulda packed up and moved to Australia when I had the chance."

Andy's gaze drifted away from the half-eaten shark to the darkness up the tunnel. Whatever did that was huge. And it happened as the smaller one clamped onto Sully. So, that meant it was still out there. Could it be waiting? Watching them? Did sharks do that? He knew they stalked prey, but—

"Hey, so, can we get the shark off me now?" Sully asked.

Andy stared into the darkness for another few seconds and swam to help Ben pry the jaws open enough for Sully to slip free. Luckily, none of the teeth punctured the suit. Sully moved to look at the dead shark and whistled.

"One'o the big bastards, for sure."

"How'd it get through with the other one being so big?" Andy said. "There wouldn't be any room."

"Aye." Sully looked at the half-eaten goblin shark that could've killed him. "It's big. Might come back to finish its meal. We need to get outta here."

"I thought sharks couldn't swim backwards," Andy said.

"They can't, but it might have drifted back a bit. It's hiding, I think. We need t'go."

Andy agreed and they boosted away at mild speed. Ben remained at Andy's side most of the time. He didn't say much, nor did he ask for his gun back. Which was good, and potentially bad. What was he planning? Or, was he done being the assassin and sticking close to Andy and Sully in a possible way to get out of the tunnels? Andy didn't ask the man, nor did he think too much about it. His mind was too strung out to hold onto any concrete idea. It reeled and bashed itself against a mirror repeatedly, his mind. It twisted and frayed.

If they didn't get out of the tunnels soon, he might very well lose his mind. He choked down a bit of panic and focused on the tunnel ahead. The unknown darkness. He—

1 NONHUMAN LIFEFORM, his visor flashed in red.

He sucked in a sharp breath, sight snapping to the red dot on the compass. His eyes widened.

"It's behind us!"

"Ah, feckin' hell," Sully said. "I hoped it wouldn't see us."

"Wait," Ben blurted. "You *knew* it was right there?"

"Sharks can't swim backwards, boyo. Told ya that. Also said it was probably just outta sight. Thought we'd get lucky. We shouldn't have much of scent and move quickly so…"

"So, instead of killing the thing, you tossed the dice to see if it'd kill us?" Ben grunted. "Nice."

"Are you mental? No." A pause. "B'sides, thought ya wouldn't wanna kill it. You bein' sensitive to animals'n'all."

"Shut up," Ben shouted. "It's different when it's a fight to survive."

"Uh-huh," Sully said. "Sure, big guy. Sure."

"Knock it off," Andy said. "Both of you. We have a giant goblin shark about to eat us, for Christ sake."

"The hell we supposed to do," Sully said, "stop'n'let it eat us?"

"No," Andy said. "We need a plan."

"Right," Ben said. "Like what?"

His gaze ventured away from the darkness ahead to the…

"The walls. Go to the walls and get as low as you can. Floor, if possible."

No one argued, so he figured the plan was a winner.

"On my word," Andy said. He waited for a couple of seconds, and, "Go!"

He shot to the right wall, aiming for the tunnel's floor.

"Shit, shit, shit," Sully spouted.

"It's—oh my G—" Ben didn't finish and by the time Andy was near the floor and turned around, his entire world was a gray wall as the massive creature swam by.

Sully pulled himself closer to the floor. "Nice plan, Boss. Now what?"

Andy shook his head. "Ben? Ben, you copy?"

"Oh, feck'im," Sully said. "Bastard was gonna kill us, remember?"

"We don't know that for sure," Andy said, heart hitching. "Ben, do you copy?"

The moving gray wall in front of him continued moving.

"How the feck is it so big?" Sully said. "It…it shouldn't be that big. Evolution be damned."

"How big do you think it is?" Andy asked.

"Fifty feet, at least. It just keeps going."

"I think we stumbled into the wrong place at the wrong time, man."

Andy nodded. "Could've told you that about an hour ago."

"Aye."

Eventually, the monstrous shark glided and gave him a view of halfway across the tunnel. He didn't spot Ben anywhere.

"Ben?"

No answer.

"He's gone," Sully said. "Fecker either doublin' to meet with his comrades, or he's gonna sneak up and—"

"Hey, guys."

"God*damn* it, ya feckin' jackass," Sully shouted. "'Bout pissed m'self."

Andy sighed relief when Ben drifted up beside Sully. The man might've been on the wrong side, but that didn't mean he was a bad guy. So far, anyway. Probably best to keep the guard up, but Andy sincerely didn't see a need. Ben seemed genuine, regardless of his past affiliations. Then again, for all Andy knew, Ben was playing them both right now and waiting for his chance to take them out.

He snuck up on us right there, Andy thought. *Came out of nowhere. Like a ghost.*

"Sorry," Ben said and gave Sully a thumbs up. "I about got run over by that thing. Dove straight down and—"

"Why didn't you answer when I radioed?" Andy asked.

"I'll show you why." Ben swam toward the middle of the tunnel.

Andy and Sully glanced at each other and followed.

Ben looked around while he floated a few inches above the floor. "Christ, you guys take forever."

"Yeah, yeah," Sully said. "Not all of us are so gung-ho to die, ya know?"

"There's nothing around us right now," Ben said.

"Yeah. We all saw how quickly that shit changes."

"Why are we here?" Andy said and spread his arms out and when he brought them down, leveled his gun on Ben. "There's nothing here. No more games."

"Games? For fuck sake, man, *look*." He pointed at the floor of the tunnel.

Andy blinked. "What…"

"Where the hell did that come from?" Sully asked.

"I don't know," Ben said. "But it saved my life."

Directly below Ben was a rather large hole in the stony floor. At least twenty feet in diameter.

"Looks like it goes pretty deep," Ben said. "Might be another tunnel. Maybe we can avoid the sharks and Guerra's men."

To Andy's surprise, Sully didn't say anything.

Andy nodded. "We'll check it out."

"I bet it—"

Andy cut Ben off. "But I want you to lead us." He needed to keep an eye on the man and cursed himself for fumbling that fact earlier. Keeping Ben front and center and a gun on him would've been the smarter plan.

Everything happened so fast.

"Okay?" Ben said. "I thought you were the—"

"I am," Andy said. "And I want you to go ahead of us."

Silence trickled in.

Andy sighed and pointed one of the guns at Ben. "It's not a request."

"Oh, shit," Sully crooned. "Someone's on someone else's shitlist."

"No shit-list," Andy said. "He was hired to kill us. Now I need to make sure he doesn't."

"Fair enough," Sully said.

"Fair?" Ben said. "*Really*? This is *fair*? Look, Brent was my target. Made to look like an accident. None of you were supposed to die by me, or otherwise. Guerra's men are there for cleanup. Nothing more. They weren't sent to kill you, but to make sure Brent was dead. They need confirmation that he's dead." Ben sighed and looked away. "They won't stop coming after us until they have that evidence."

"Can't ya tell 'em a big feckin' shark ate the poor bastard?"

"They've already heard all about it. Just like they hear all of this. They know, even Guerra knows, but they still need the evidence. They need something proving Brent is dead."

Andy shrugged. "They should have all the evidence they need just by listening."

"Ya don't get it," Sully said. "The Cartel is fuckin' mad. They wanna make damn sure there aren't any loose ends."

"Not mad, or crazy, but calculating and concise. Guerra is the most intelligent drug lord I've ever met. He's cunning and more than a little paranoid. If a millimeter of mistrust squirms in him, he'll kill you. And it doesn't matter now. He'll be coming for all our heads."

"Yeah," Andy said and motioned for Ben to move ahead. "We'll figure it out. Need to keep moving."

Ben sighed and swam a few feet in front of Andy.

"Less room to move around down here," Andy said. "Just in case, we should keep it slow. Ben, I want you to mild boost. Sully and I will keep steady on low."

"Do I get a gun now?" Ben asked.

Sully snorted, "Does a penguin fly?"

Ben said nothing and told the suit to mild boost. He scooted on ahead a few meters. Suits set to low boost, Andy and Sully followed.

CHAPTER 21

The new tunnel was constrictive compared to the main tunnel above. The current was also stronger. It pushed them along a couple of knots faster than the booster propelled them. And when the tunnel turned, it took more than just leaning in the right direction. Andy had to use his arms to keep from crashing into the smooth walls.

"Tell me again why we're in this death tube?" Sully said.

"Because it's not as dangerous as the one above."

Sully snorted. "Well, not so far, aye."

"How you doing up there, Ben?" Andy called.

"Fine. Current sucks. But fine."

The shadows swelled around them. Claustrophobia jabbed at Andy's guts like the pointy tines of a pitchfork. He groaned, fighting to keep himself from freaking out.

"You okay, Boss?" Sully asked.

"Y-Yeah. Just, this tunnel is too cramped for me."

"Aye. Me too. Know what I do when I get a touch'o'the claustrophobia?"

"What?"

"Think 'bout m'kiddos."

Andy glanced at the Irishman. "You have kids?"

"Look, I know I'm this exotic little birdie to ya, but aye. Got two boys."

"I have a boy and a girl."

"Lucky bastard," Sully said. "The two boyos are—"

"You two done?" Ben interrupted. "Something's up ahead. Not sure what it is."

Jarred out of the moment, Andy's attention returned to the tunnel. His visor blipped red for a second or two, then it was gone. Other than that, he didn't see anything.

"The hell ya goin' on 'bout?" Sully said. "I don't see anything."

"Did your visor go red for like a second or two?"

"Aye. Probably a glitch."

"Not a glitch if we all saw it," Ben said.

"I saw it," Andy said.

Ben made a good point. If they all saw it, it probably wasn't a glitch. Unless it was a universal glitch due to the linking system, well, then maybe. Still the questions bobbing around in his mind came to: What's out there? What's waiting?

Maybe whatever was out there was too small to fully detect. A hope soon thought in vain when they found it.

"Slow booster," they said in near unison.

"Stop," Andy said. The other two followed quickly behind.

It twitched in the black water. The large, ancient creature floating before them didn't attack. Rather, it floated and twitched sporadically. It twisted and writhed, blood clouding around its snapping mouth. Andy gaped at it, not really sure what to do.

"She was attacked too," Sully said, moving bit closer. "Bit a chunk out of'er. Not dead yet, though."

Andy could see it all, though remained quiet. He surveyed the situation. The way the large, dying goblin shark twitched and snapped. How much blood obscured most of its body.

"Where's the thing that bit into it?" Andy asked. And, when no one answered, "Be alert. It's somewhere around here."

"Might've been a hit'n'run," Sully said while they watched the dying goblin shark twitch its final twitch and sink to the tunnel's floor. "The bite isn't from one of the monsters up there, though. Radius is too small. Aye, it was something—"

Something shot out of the shadows to the right and crashed into the dead goblin shark. It tore into the corpse with serious and bloody vigor.

"Holy shit," Ben said. He joined Andy and Sully.

"Tiger," Sully said in a calm tone. "Fecker got lost in here too. Not supposed to be so deep, though. Fifteen hundred feet is thought t'be their max.

"Tiger," Andy said. "As in tiger shark?"

"Aye. What else? She's a bit hungry too."

Andy gaped while the tiger shark ripped through the goblin. "A bit?"

"Aye. A wee bit. Anyhoo, we should kill'er and keep movin'."

"We don't need to kill it," Ben said.

"Oh, *now* you care about life again," Sully spat. "The feck were ya killin' the other gobbies, then?"

"Shut up," Ben said. "It was us or them at the time. This is different. It just wants to eat. Poor thing has probably been starving down here for a while."

"Probably," Sully said. "But it'll attack ya just like the gobbies. What then?"

"We'll see."

Andy watched the tiger shark devour the goblin in a pink cloud and bits of pale flesh. "High boost by it. We'll be moving too fast for it to react."

"Maybe," Sully said. "She's ravenous right now."

"We'll try anyway."

Sully sighed. "Aye. Let's go."

"It came from the right. Might be a tributary. Go right. Rapid boost," Andy said and shot forward and away from the carnage in less than two seconds.

The other two told their suits the same.

The tiger shark didn't notice.

There was indeed a tributary on the right. Though they soon came to realize it was a deep cave. Something large enough for the tiger shark to turn around in and finish off the goblin.

"Shit," Andy said and turned back to the way they came. "Okay. Back to the tunnel. Go to the mouth of the tunnel and rapid boost to the right again."

They drifted to the mouth of the cave. Andy peered out and gaped at the massive cloud of pink water about twenty feet away. He couldn't see the tiger shark through all the mess so slipped around the corner and faced the darkness. The tunnel, he hoped, would lead to a way out.

"Rapi—"

It struck his back hard enough to drive him forward a few meters. Before he could move, he was being thrashed around like a rottweiler's ragdoll.

"Ah, feck," Sully muttered.

Andy's world became a blurred mess. He tried to tell the suit to rapid boost, but his words came out too jumbled for the suit to recognize.

Goddamn it, he thought.

Pain spread throughout his back. Not from teeth, at least he hoped not, but from the initial strike. If he made it out of this, he'd have one hell of a bruise.

"Hold on, boyo," Sully said. "Takin' aim. I gotcha pal."

Andy drew in a breath and closed his eyes. If the Irishman missed...

The thrashing stopped.

"M-Mild boost." The suit didn't react. Andy cursed himself. "Mild boost." The suit shot forward at around twenty miles per hour. Once he was clear, he said, "Stop." Instead of jarring, he drifted to a stop. Which was a relief. His stomach was a tumbling mess.

"Damn," Ben said. "You okay, Andy?"

He glanced from Ben to the sinking tiger shark and shook his head. "Didn't realize how hard they hit."

"Aye," Sully said. "They pack quite the punch. Whities get all the media attention. Rightly so. Big feckers. But in the Gulf and Caribbean, tigers are deadlier. They don't care. They just attack and eat everything."

Andy stared at the dead tiger shark. "We need to get out of here."

"What was y'first clue, Boss?"

The tunnel seemed to run directly below the main one. Andy hated how close the walls were. Hated the feeling of not having much room to move if they ran into something larger than the tiger shark. Hated everything about the situation.

Weariness stole over him and all he wanted to do was float there. Right then, he didn't care if something devoured him. He didn't care if the Cartel blew dozens of holes into him. It all felt so damn hopeless.

Right then, Andy almost gave up.

But it was a fleeting feeling.

His mind turned to his kids. They needed him to make it. They needed him to live.

Andy straightened and said, "Let's get outta here."

"Hey," Sully said. "Didn't you say that earlier? We're still here, boyo…"

With a sigh, Andy shook his head and faced the darkness of the tunnel. "Ben, just stick close. Sully, give him his gun back.

"Wait, what?" Sully said. "The fecker will kill us."

"If I wanted to kill you," Ben said, "I would've done earlier while you were distracted by the shark."

An uneasy silence fell between them all for a few seconds.

"Fine," Sully said, sounding more than a little pissed off. "But I want you in front of me.'

"You just wanna look at my butt."

"I just—*no*! Goddamn it, man. What's wrong with ya? Here, take the feckin' gun and go away. Weird bastard."

Ben brayed laughter and Andy chuckled. Even if Sully was legitimately upset, the outburst seemed to form a loose unity between the three. At least, Andy hoped so.

He also hoped he wasn't wrong about Ben.

Andy gripped his gun and said, "Rapid boost."

CHAPTER 22

The tunnel twisted and turned without an end in sight.

There were no sharks.

No life of any kind.

What stretched out before Andy was a vast, eternal darkness. One, no matter how far he traveled, would never come to an end. Once more, that hopelessness invaded his mind.

A failure...

What if there wasn't a way out now? What if they were trapped down here until they died of thirst? There were too many what ifs and it terrified the hell out of him. The unknown could unnerve even the most stoic person. Indeed, it was what drove most people mad.

"We should've stuck to the main tunnel," Ben said.

"So your Cartel bastards could find us easier?" Sully said. "Yeah, how 'bout nah."

"Every tunnel has a beginning and end," Andy said, recalling an article about cave diving some years ago. "Just keep moving." If the article was legit or not, well...they were about to find out.

The tunnel took a hard left. A damn near ninety-degree angle.

"Low boost," Andy shouted when he noticed the abrupt change and the other two said the same.

Not a moment too soon.

Andy about crashed into the wall of the curve and shifted just enough to follow it around.

"Stop," he said, and the suit stopped.

"St—ah feck," Sully shouted.

Andy turned around in time to watch Sully crash into the wall and bounce back, resulting in Ben crashing into him. Then they both collided with the wall. A complete clusterfuck.

"G'damnit," Sully said. "Get off me, ya big bastard."

"Why didn't you move?" Ben said.

Andy sighed and said, "The curve came up fast. Stop bickering."

"Bickerin'?" Sully said. "More like gettin' ready to go off on m'own and let ya both bumble'round down here."

"What's stopping you?" Ben said.

"Shit, I dunno. Maybe 'cause I kinda like Andy? Reminds m'of m'oldest daughter."

"Girly?"

"No, ya dumb bastard. Born a leader but doesn't know it yet."

Andy snorted. "If I'm a leader, you two sure as hell don't listen very well."

Sully made a clucking sound. "Well, I be testin' ya. Makin' ya great, ya know?"

Even Ben chuckled. Or, at least Andy thought he did.

"Okay," Andy said. The tunnel ahead appeared to be even narrower than the last. About ten feet in diameter. Maybe less.

He frowned at the smooth walls, gaze drifting back and forth. No. He couldn't do it. It was too narrow. The walls were too close. He couldn't—

"Ya know," Sully said and swam to Andy's right side, "ya do this every time we come to a new tunnel. Makes m'wonder if ya might be claustrophobic."

Andy spun on the Irishman. "I don't..." He sighed. "Okay, maybe a little."

"Right," Sully said. "Thought so. Had a mate like that. Ya know what got him through the Army?"

Andy shook his head.

"He kept looking straight on. Didn't look around him. Just focused on what lay ahead. T'was the only thing that kept him from goin' stark mad'n'shankin' us all."

"Right," Andy said, trying to focus straight ahead. Trying to ignore the walls.

The more he stared down the tunnel, though not being able to see much beyond one hundred feet, the better he felt. Well, at least a little. Enough to ease his rampaging heart, anyway. He drew in a breath and blew it out slow. Okay...

"Let's go," Andy said.

They boosted down the narrower tunnel. Andy glared straight ahead. He felt the walls there, but Sully's advice, at least for now, was working. That's what mattered. Ahead, the tunnel appeared to widen. He just needed to get through the—

"Holy shit," Ben said. "Andy, *stop!*"

If not for either Sully or Ben grabbing him, he would've been in serious trouble.

The tunnel opened to a vast cavern. From what he could tell, it was where all the tunnels led to. Even the smaller tributaries. But that's not what grabbed him by the throat and clamped down.

Not far below were dozens, if not hundreds of goblin sharks. They swam in what made Andy think of as a giant cylinder. And yet, they didn't appear to only be swimming. It looked like they were trying to kill each other. Some of them thrashed around, blood turning the water scarlet. And they were massive. As large as the one that ate Brent whole. Some, perhaps, even larger. Andy's equilibrium swayed and he fought the urge to faint. Something he had never done before.

The sensation passed and he backed away from the ledge of the tunnel's mouth.

"Y-You guys see them?" Andy managed.

"Aye," Sully said.

"Yeah," Ben said.

"Aye, you were right," Sully said. "We're in breedin' grounds."

"Shit," Ben said. "You sure?"

"No. Those two gobbies are jus'thrashin'round for no reason. Dumb fecker."

"Look," Ben said, "I don't know what the hell sharks do when—"

"I told you about the nurse sharks in the shallows, ya arse. Trust me. They're all here t'bang."

Silence swept through the trio.

Andy frowned. Why was it slightly lighter in the cavern? Something he noted, though didn't really think about until now. He saw farther down than he should have been able to. Not a cavern, but a giant hole, it went on forever, from what he could see between the frenzy of huge goblin sharks. There were so many of them. Too many.

"Hey," Sully said and pointed. "Look up there."

Andy followed the Irishman's finger and blinked at a small, but large enough hole in the ceiling of the cavern. A small ray of light shone through the hole. Nothing much, but large enough to light the cavern up some. That's why it was lighter here than the tunnels.

"Looks like a way out," Andy said, mostly to himself.

"Aye. Gotta be 'bout six feet wide, I'd say. We can fit through."

"Yeah," Ben said, "but what about them?" He pointed at the thrashing sexcapades in the cylindrical cavern.

"Gobbies are slow," Sully said. "Even the big ones. We can boost right on outta here and they'd never notice. Gotta be quick."

Andy nodded. "Okay. That's what we do, then. Single file, rapid boost." His heart stuttered when one of the huge goblin sharks glided by. A shiver ran through him like ice water.

If Sully was right, the hole in the cavern's ceiling might be their only way out.

He focused on the ragged hole above. "On three. One. Two. Thre—"

One of the other men screamed.

Andy spun around, but at first his brain wouldn't grasp what was happening. The water began turning scarlet.

"Motherfucker," Ben roared amid flashes of light as a rifle went off.

It wasn't Ben who was screaming, though.

It was Sully.

By the time Andy's brain caught up with what his eyes were telling it, Sully stopped screaming. A shark, not a goblin, but what appeared to be another great white, had Sully's leg in its mouth, thrashing back and forth like an old cloth doll. Ben moved back and forth, putting bullets into the shark's head.

Andy lifted his own rifle and—

The great white shot forward and shoved them all out of the tunnel. It released Sully and Andy grabbed the Irishman before he could sink into the giant, thrashing goblin sharks. He used a stabilizing boost to keep them afloat.

"Ah, shit," Ben said. "Where'd it go?"

The cavern clouded with blood, making it difficult to see anything.

"We need to get to the hole," Andy said, terror ripping through him like a buzz saw. "W-We're in the cavern now."

"I can't even see where it is."

"Boost straight up," Andy said. "We need to get away from all the blood."

In Andy's arms, Sully groaned and relief spilled through Andy. The guy wasn't dead after all. At least, not yet. There wasn't any time to see if the shark's teeth broke through the suit either. Though, if they had, Sully would have drowned by now.

"Rapid boost," Andy said and the thrusters in his boots jetted him upward like a rocket man…

…and directly into something large he hadn't seen above. He struck the object, about lost Sully, and redirected himself to the right side.

"Where'd you go?" Ben called. "I can't see anything."

"Something above us. Rapid boost to the right. Once we're out of the blood, aim for that hole."

"Gotcha," Ben said. "I just—"

Silence.

Andy frowned, trying to keep his gaze focused for any shadows in the cloud of blood. Especially anything that would bite. "Ben?"

Nothing but silence.

"Ben? You copy?"

No response.

"Best get movin'," Sully said. "We're in the feckin' cavern now. Big gobbies."

Andy cried out and about let Sully go.

"Settle down, boyo," Sully said. "Not sure what happened back there. Just passed out. Couldn't breathe."

Andy glanced at the man. "How long have you been awake?"

"Oh…" Sully said. "'Bout when we were pushed out of the tunnel."

Andy let the Irishman go and said, "Low boost." To Sully, he said, "Ben isn't answering."

"Aye," Sully said. "Heard that."

"Are you hurt?"

Sully didn't even pause. "Nah. Bruised up, b'not bad."

"Good."

"Only problem I got, though," Sully said, "somethin' cold'n'wet is spraying my leg."

Andy gasped. He couldn't help it. "You're taking on water?"

"Aye. I mean, maybe?"

With a low growl in his throat, Andy grabbed Sully's arm and boosted them upward and out of the cloud of blood. He needed to get Sully out of the water before the guy drowned. With the pressure, the tiny hole letting in water could burst wide open in no time. Andy was a little shocked it hadn't yet. Perhaps it was but a pinprick. Even so, a pinhole could become a two-foot gash in less than a minute if given the right circumstances.

Unless…they weren't as deep as Andy originally thought…

No time to dwell on that now.

"Let's get out of here," Andy said, as he grabbed Sully's free arm and sighed relief when the cloud dissipated some, clearing the view to the hole in the ceiling. "Rapid boost."

Arms linked, Andy and Sully shot upward toward the hole. The opening in the ceiling. Toward the light. Toward freedom.

Forty meters to the opening.

Thirty.

Twenty.

Ten.

It crashed into them with so much force Andy didn't even know what happened until he collided into a rock pillar. Everything became a flurry of agony for a bit until a monstrous shark cruised by. That great wall of gray he was unfortunately getting used to drifted by.

"Andy?" Sully said. "Stick close t'somethin' solid. They're gonna be in a frenzy now. Stay still."

"How's the leak?" Andy moved and gritted his teeth. When he struck the pillar of rock it jostled his body a bit inside the suit. He was going to be more bruise than man if he made it out of this. "Can you breathe okay?"

"Aye. Jus' fine. Now hush. Once the gobbies settle down, we make for the opening."

Andy's gaze slinked to the hole in the ceiling. "Where's the other shark? The great white?"

"Was that what got me?" Sully snorted. "Well, shit."

"Right. But have you seen it?"

"Nah. One o'the gobbies got'er I'm sure."

Andy leaned against the rock pillar, heart bashing into his ribs. Sully didn't know where the great white was. Even with a few rounds in its head, the damn thing was still going strong. A sudden current pulled him to the right. He turned the low boost on and pulled away in time for the largest goblin shark yet to swim in front of him. A true monster. At least fifty feet long. Maybe more.

It glided by and he had to move around the rock pillar before its tail crashed into him.

Still, he was more concerned about the great white. His gaze scanned a huge goblin shark, but they were moving too erratically and frenzied to see through them. The cloud of blood had nearly dissipated already.

Sully was right. They needed to wait. Too much craziness going on and…

Sully coughed. Then coughed again.

"You okay?"

"Aye," Sully said. "Don't ever fart in these things. Gah…"

Despite their situation, Andy burst out laughing.

"Aye. Glad you're all amused over there but I think a rat crawled up in here'n'died."

Once Andy was able to catch his breath, he managed, "We're in the ocean!"

Sully grunted. "Sea rats, boyo."

That garnered another bout of laughter. Not that it was really that funny, but sometimes a good laugh helped relieve stress. It got a person back on track.

And, sometimes, it led to utter madness.

Andy didn't know which it'd be, but he grasped for the stress card. Images of his kids floated by his mind's eye. No. He couldn't go insane. He needed to make it back to them. The mere thought of their smiling faces reignited the need to push onward.

There was no sign of the great white and the goblin sharks began bumping uglies again.

He couldn't see Sully on the other side of the cavern. Or, at least from midway. The cavern was enormous, after all and Andy harbored no illusions to the fact.

"Let's go," Andy said. "Rapid boost the opening."

"Aye. On three?"

"No. Now. Rapid boost."

He shot upward toward the hole in the ceiling. The opening he hoped would lead him back to his children.

"Rapid boost," Sully said, sounding weak and rundown.

Andy jetted toward the opening and hoped Sully wasn't far behind him. The Irishman was taking on water. Only a matter of time now. They needed to get him out of the ocean before the suit either split open or filled up with water.

The hole in the ceiling grew larger the closer he got to it. At least ten feet at its widest. Nothing round, but more like a ragged oval. An open eye staring down at him.

"Almost there," Andy said.

"Aye. I see it. Comin' up on ya here to your right."

Andy glanced to find the Irishman shooting toward him. He didn't dare look below at the monsters that swam there. He returned his attention to the opening in the ceiling. Triumph spilled through him in joyful waves of bright colors. Only a few feet from the hole now.

He looked at Sully, who gave him a thumbs up—a mouth with teeth at least a foot long snapped onto Sully at mid torso.

"No," Andy shouted as Sully was yanked backward and out of sight.

"Mild boost." The suit slowed. "Low boost." The suit crawled along.

He was only about three feet from the opening. Three feet to freedom. Three feet closer to his kids.

"Stop," Andy said and turned to face the massive sharks. "Sully?"

There was no scream. No sounds at all.

Below lay shifting darkness. A darkness that couldn't be trusted.

"Sully do you copy?"

"G-get outta here, ya stupid fecker."

Relief trickled through Andy, though only for a moment. "Not without you."

"Y'can't, boyo. Inside the fecker, I think. Somethin's stingin'm'leg too. Stomach acid, maybe."

Andy's heart trip-hammered. "You're *inside* it? Can you shoot your way out?"

"Nah. Lost m'gun. Get outta here and take care o' your kiddos."

Tears prickled Andy's eyes. "What about yours?"

"Ah, they'll be fine. Got their mum in Ireland. They get my pension too."

"I can try to get you out."

"Yeah? Which shark am I in? Probably dozens of 'em right? Which one? Ya don't have enough bullets to kill 'em all, boyo."

Andy's gaze drifted over the mating sharks. The one that got Sully was huge. Larger than any of the others he encountered. So...where...?

"Ya gone, yet?" Sully said. "Better be."

Andy turned to the hole, then back to the roiling mess of giant goblin sharks. Mating. Or so Sully said. As Andy had thought, the tunnels were like breeding grounds.

They were in the wrong place at the wrong time. That much was clear. The wrong tunnels system, for sure.

"I can't just leave you," Andy said.

"The feck ya can't," Sully spouted. "Go now, m'friend. See ya in the next one, aye?"

Andy released a breath too heavy to be a sigh. "Yeah. Yeah. See you in the next one, man."

"Go take care'o'those kiddos."

Andy nodded, "I will." He went to leave and stopped. Not really wanting to tell Sully what needed to be said but doing so anyway. Because, that's what friends did. "The suit has a self-destruct option. Was implemented in case of infectious diseases or if you happened into an oil slick. It will give you ten minutes to get clear of it before it blows. But since you can't exactly get out…" He left it hanging there for a couple of seconds. Ominous and gray. "Just order it to self-destruct."

"Aye. Live well, Andy. Live well."

"See you, again, man."

Sounding far away and sad, Sully said, "Aye, boyo. Aye."

Jaw clenched, Andy turned and mild boosted out of the cavern.

CHAPTER 23

Free of the tunnels and cavern, Andy found himself lost both physically and emotionally. He stopped the thrusters and simply floated for a while in the deep, black waters of the Gulf of Mexico.

He fought the tears, but they came anyway. They spilled down his cheeks and Andy was unable to wipe them away. For some reason, that was the worst part. He couldn't wipe the tears away. He couldn't fucking do anything. He was trapped in the damned thing. The suit. The very thing keeping him alive was also killing him. Breaking him down, bit by bit.

Images shuffled through his mind like playing cards. Images of everyone who died in the tunnels. Of Sully. Of Genson.

Of his children…

A shiver trickled through him and eventually, he found north and told the suit to, "Rapid boost."

Then everything went to hell.

Something struck him from below hard enough to boost him without the boosters upward. Pressure clamped down over his right leg. He cried out, trying to fight whatever was thrashing him around enough to kick it and speed away. Surely the rapid boost would outrun whatever had him.

He caught a glimpse or two of the monster shaking him back and forth so vigorously. It was all he needed.

The great white he thought dead whipped him back and forth. The pressure on his leg increased to the point of hurting. If a tooth broke through, he'd be in the same situation as Sully. Taking on water and exposed to the deep sea. Terror ripped through him at the very thought and he was able to sway the thrashing just enough to put a bullet into the great white's eye. A lucky shot. It released him and he boosted around, crazy.

"Mild boost," Andy said, rage filling him. "Low boost." He had one thing to do before leaving. A bit of revenge, perhaps.

Andy turned back to the great white shark. It writhed, blood pluming from the fresh wound where its eye had been. Even so, it soon stilled and focused on Andy again.

"Shit," he said and pointed the rifle at the shark.

It shot forward and Andy squeezed the trigger, emptying the magazine into the shark. By the time the mag was dry, the water swirled with blood.

Gotta get away from the blood, he thought, turning to rapid boost away. *Gotta g—*

Something struck him with so much force it sent him pinwheeling out of the large cloud of blood.

"Stabilize," he told the suit, but it didn't comply. Flipping now, over and over, he tried again. "Stabilize!"

The suit beeped and gradually righted itself. The halt, though gradual, still jarred Andy enough to have him frowning at nothing for some unknown length of time. When everything finally clicked together, he gaped at a large mouth lined with long, pointy teeth shooting toward him.

"Rapid boost," he shouted and jetted straight up, barely avoiding the snapping jaws.

He looked down, but couldn't see anything, so slowed to low boost. The submersible rifle was empty. He had no form of protection.

Just go, he thought. *Sully said they were slow.*

Yes, but—

He turned just in time to catch a silver glint about forty meters out. Andy frowned, watching the shiny silver object. In a handful of seconds, he drew in a long breath. His eyes widened.

It was Guerra's men in another sub. Had to be.

"Fuck," Andy said and glanced around.

The giant goblin shark was nowhere to be seen. Maybe it ate the great white and that was good enough. Andy returned his attention to the approaching minisub. There was nowhere to go. Nowhere to hide. He could try to rapid boost away, but if they had missiles or mounted guns, he'd be screwed anyway. So, he faced the small sub. He faced the men who were sent to Brent and the team.

Time for a reckoning.

He would be dead either way.

Images of his kids shuffled before his mind's eye. He smiled and fought tears. The early Christmas mornings when they woke to presents from Santa. Summer evenings around a campfire while the gentle waves of a lake lapped at the beach and the call of a loon. Simply hanging out in the living room while some movie or another played on the TV, no matter how much they paid attention. It was just amazing to have them close. Andy loved no one more than his own kids. So many memories and predictions like his son and daughter growing up and having children of their own. Grandchildren.

You're too young to be thinking about grandchildren, Andy thought. But, was he? Especially with death facing him head on and lurking below? It was like life flashing before his eyes, only years in the future. It was both weird and comforting for reasons he wasn't quite sure of.

He drew in a breath and blew it out slowly as the minisub approached. Once they spotted him, it'd all be over. He hoped his kids would be taken care of. He hoped—

It happened so fast Andy didn't have time to breathe.

The massive head of a goblin shark rose up below the minisub. Its slingshot jaws snatched the thing, like a frog with a dragonfly, and pulled it into its mouth.

Andy blinked, and watched the giant shark glide by and head back toward the deep without even sparing a glance at him.

Go, he told himself. *Now!* Andy positioned himself to rapid boost away from everything and not stop until he reached shore. Before he could say a word, something latched onto both his legs. He glanced back and would have screamed if he had the voice. It had him, the huge goblin shark that ate Guerra's minisub. Pain spread through his thighs and settled into his groin and lower abdomen. That's how much pressure those monstrous jaws produced and hoped to whatever god was out there that the teeth hadn't punctured the suit.

It didn't waste time, either.

Those jaws sucked him into the mouth itself.

"Gone a few minutes'n'ya get yourself eaten," Sully said. "The feckin' hell, boyo?"

Andy opened his mouth, though words defied him.

"Get ready to rapid boost, lad."

Andy wanted to say something, *anything*, but he still couldn't find his voice. No matter how much he tried, all that would come out was a faint whine. He struggled not to get sucked down into the shark.

"On three," Sully said. "One. Two. Three!"

All at once, Andy got tossed around inside the monster's mouth.

"She's hurt," Sully said. "Give me another three." When Andy didn't respond, he shouted, "Still alive, ya fecker?"

Andy jolted back to himself. "I, uh, yeah. Sorry, everything happened so fast."

"Aye. Count t'three, boyo."

Still being tossed around inside the mouth, Andy counted. "One. T-Two. Thr—"

The jaws opened, extending at the same time.

"Now," Sully cried.

"Rapid boost!"

Andy blasted out of the open mouth and shot away from the shark at least sixty feet before slowing and stopping. He turned back.

"Sully," he said. "You okay?"

"Aye," Sully said. "She's not, though."

The massive shark wriggled about like a latex minnow on a fisherman's jig. "I don't have any ammo."

"Can't b'helped," Sully said. "She won't mind either. Pumped a dozen rounds into her head. Mild boost."

In a short time, Sully joined Andy and they watched the huge goblin shark twitch before finally sinking into the depths.

Andy shivered and faced Sully. "How'd you get out of the shark?"

The Irishman chuckled. "Y'know these suits have lasers?"

"What? No, I was never told…maybe it's an upgrade? I thought these were older models."

"Anyway," Sully said. "There is. Found'er b'accident. Y'know, if ya make a fist in these things, there's a bit of a nub by the end of y'palm? Not far from the wrist?"

Andy tried it and soon discovered the nub Sully was talking about. More like a tiny button his middle finger probed.

"Shoots out the top of your forearm," Sully said. "Go ahead and pop a beam, boyo."

"Pop a b—what does that even mean?"

Sully sighed. "Try'er out, fecker."

Andy pointed his arm at the dark sea in front of him and pressed the tiny button near his wrist. Almost like a Spider-Man. A greenish beam shot out. The water boiled around it. He lifted his finger and the beam vanished.

"Used that to cut'er open and get out," Sully said. "Y'should feel lucky, I did."

Andy nodded. "I am. Thank you."

"Aye." Sully grunted. "Best get outta the water. Getting harder to breathe'n'm'leg still burns."

Andy nodded. "Let's go."

CHAPTER 24

"Guerra's men were inside the shark you killed. I think." Andy's gaze lifted to the top of his visor. "In a minisub."

They jetted through the water at about two hundred feet deep. The compass in Andy's visor told him they were heading due north. It didn't matter where they came ashore now. What did was getting there.

"Aye," Sully said. "Saw it happen. They'll tear their way out. But we're long gone from there. They'd need some kinda warp drive or radio ahead to their mates."

Andy thought about that a for a bit, and said, "Either or is possible."

"Aye. It is. It is indeed…"

Andy huffed out a breath and forced himself not to look behind him. No point in it. Better to just keep moving. Keep blasting through the Gulf's water and reach shore. After that, well…he wasn't sure. Maybe find a way to meet up with Angela Wexler.

In a game where both bosses were bad, the choice was a lesser of both evils. Guerra would kill them both, so, Wexler it was.

Unless…unless they just disappeared? Maybe get their families together and create new identities. That might be better than—

"Gettin' harder t'breathe, boyo," Sully said.

Andy glanced at the visor's upper left curve. It read 20 MILES.

"We only have twenty more miles till shore," Andy said. "You think you can make it? If we have to surface, then so be it."

"Aye," Sully said with a heavy breath. "Think I might be alright."

Andy didn't believe one word of it. As weak as the man's voice was and the heavy breathing. The guy was on the verge of suffocation.

"We're surfacing."

"No," Sully said. "We'll be seen by predators more than we are now, not to mention Guerra's men."

"If we don't," Andy said, "you'll drown."

"What are y'plannin' on pushin' me along now? Me with no helmet. perhaps? Waste'o'time, boyo. W-Wast'o'time."

That last sounded even weaker than before. Sully was fighting it. Trying to be tough. Andy had known men like Sully all his life, including old Genson. They knew they were hurt but tried their damnedest not to show it to other people. The type of people who would rather wrestle a wolverine than tell a doctor about the blood in the toilet bowl, or the pain shooting down their left arm.

"We'll have to unlock your visor," Andy said, "so you can breathe. It's our only option."

"Ha," Sully said. "It's your option. I…" He drew in a heavy breath and blew it out in a shuddery mess. "I'll b'fine till shore. Twenty miles ain't long."

Anger flared within Andy. "Look, I couldn't stop the shark from eating you, but I can stop this. You're going to the surface. You're going to live to see your kids again."

Sully chuckled. "You're a persistent lil'fecker, aren't ya?"

Andy smiled. They zoomed by a couple of sea turtles and some shiny fish he didn't know the name of. "Thought you would've figured that out before now."

"I knew I hated ya for a reason." Sully chuckled once more, coughed a bit. "'K, boyo. Y'win. Surface it is."

Andy sighed relief and smiled. "Good. Let's slow to mild boost and surface."

"Hopefully it's not very choppy up there."

"Mild boost," Andy said, aiming himself upward. "Only one way to find ou—what—"

It barreled into him. A large, dark creature. It tossed him aside like a bull with an inept fighter. Andy flipped around until he got the suit to stabilize.

"Andy?" Sully called. "Y'okay?"

Heart thundering, Andy said, "Yeah. You see what hit me?"

"Nah. Was headed to the surface when it came through'n'hit ya. Moved too fast. Might've been a spooked shark."

Controlling the blasting of his heart, Andy said, "What the hell would be big enough to spook a shark that size?"

"Probably the one my visor is freaking out about," Sully said.

Andy frowned, noted the direction Sully faced, and turned. His visor lit up red with the words: LARGE NONHUMAN LIFEFORM – 100 FEET.

"It never lit up so bright in the tunnel," Sully said.

"Maybe those were juvenile?"

Andy blinked at the massive dark figure growing larger and larger in front of him. "Wha—What the fuck is that?"

Sully didn't say anything for a few seconds.

"I…I think it's Mama."

"What?"

"I don't know, but I think she's coming here to breed too."

Andy frowned. "Another goblin shark?"

"Aye. Maybe the oldest. Gobbies don't even get as big as those in the tunnels, as far as scientists could confirm, and they sure as hell don't get as big as this girl comin' at us."

"You have any more ammo?"

"Aye," Sully said. "Still a few rounds in the mag. Not near enough to kill'er, though."

Andy, heart hammering, said, "If we rapid boost, will that attract attention to us?"

"We'd be movin' too fast. She wouldn't notice much."

"You sure?"

"Ha! I was a marine biologist when I was a lad. Think I know some things."

It was good enough for Andy. "Does it matter which way?"

"Anywhere but up. She'll get us that way easier. Natural strike position. Somethin' like that." He coughed, wheezed. "Go right."

"Rapid boost," Andy said and jetted off to the right as the giant of giant goblin sharks made it to the thirty-foot mark.

"Rapid boost," Sully said.

The Irishman joined Andy, gave him a thumbs up and—

Sully disappeared.

"Sully?"

"Ah, shit," Sully shouted. "She's got m'boyo."

"Fuck," Andy said. "Mild boost." He turned around, not seeing Sully or the shark. "Low boost." His visor blinked red. LARGE NONHUMAN LIFEFORM 1, HUMAN LIFEFORM 1.

He still couldn't see Sully or the shark. He cruised at fifteen miles per hour in what he assumed was the right direction, but there still was no sign of either man or shark. He hated himself for not having them rapid boost away before the goblin shark got too close.

"Sully?"

A grunt. "She...she's takin' me down to the tunnels."

"Can you shoot it?"

A long pause. "Aye."

The Irishman didn't sound very convinced, though.

"Rapid boost," Andy said, aiming himself in the direction of the lifeforms. He squeezed his hand into a fist, middle finger resting over the nub, or button, rather, for the laser.

He didn't know what he was going to do. All he knew was he couldn't just let Sully die. At least, he had to try to save the man. Only a coward would let someone die if they had the means to help. Unless circumstances were dire, such as getting eaten by a massive goblin shark, people needed to help each other more.

At least that was Andy's belief on the subject.

Didn't make him right, or wrong.

But people needed to try more. They needed to stand by each other during horrific times and bland times. They needed to love each other more. If nothing changed, the world would soon perish as a result. Even so, Andy was pretty sure it was too late to stop the destruction. Humankind, he theorized, was like a disease sometimes. It kept consuming life until nothing was left but darkness.

Such darkness which awaited him one hundred and eight feet straight ahead.

CHAPTER 25

"Shot the fecker," Sully shouted. "Spent the mag'n'she's still goin'."

"Shit," Andy said. He was about eighty feet away and closing.

His depth meter read: 1,205 ft.

"Hurts," Sully said. "Gettin'…gettin' hard t'breathe."

"Just hold on," Andy said. "I'm almost there."

"She's…she's…"

Sully fell silent.

"She's what?"

No answer.

"Sully?"

Nothing but bleak silence.

Andy tried to make his body as aerodynamic as possible to move faster. For all he knew, Sully was drowning. Or, more than likely, the hole in the leg of his suit had finally opened more. Maybe Sully was already dead. Regardless, he needed to be sure.

The sea slipped by him and he didn't care. All that mattered was the titanic goblin shark that had Sully. Saving a father, like himself. A man with children waiting for him at home. He needed to at least try.

"Sh-She's takin' me too…deep," Sully said. "C-Can't breathe."

"Don't talk," Andy said. "Just try and breathe normal. I'm almost there."

Indeed, the enormous goblin shark came into view. A monster the size of a football field. At least. If not, damn near close. Something so huge Andy could barely fathom. It took a great deal to shove fear aside and continue. No matter how much his stomach churned, or his heart stammered, he boosted onward. Because, even though failing was terrifying in so many ways, at least he could die knowing he tried to do the right thing.

Andy pointed his right arm at the shark and pressed the button near his wrist. A thin, red line shot out of his forearm and sliced through half the huge goblin shark's tail. It thrashed, its tail flailing, attached by nothing but a strip of skin. There was no blood, the laser cauterized the wound instantly, though bits of burnt flesh swirled in the torrents left by the thrashing shark.

"Holy shit," Sully said. "Bein' shaken like a feckin' ragdoll."

"I…" Andy shook his head and slowed the suit to low boost. He didn't want to get too close to all that thrashing. "I cut its tail off."

"She's gonna pull me down with'er. Can't swim without a tail."

Andy drifted, not sure what to do for a moment or two until the shark flopped onto its side and he got a perfect view of Sully half in and half out of the monster's jaws. It still thrashed, trying to swim but unable to.

Every now and then, a red line would swish through the water.

"Jesus Christ," Sully said. "I can't get a good enough position to cut the fecker."

"If I cut its head off," Andy ventured, "would the jaws release?"

"Fifty-fifty, boyo. Dunno till ya do it."

Andy's jaw clenched. "Hold still, then."

"How the fuck am I supposed to hold still, ya bastard? She's going berserk here, if ya hadn't noticed."

Andy sighed. "How's the breathing?"

"Sucks. She's movin' me around like this, I can feel water sloshing up to my sack."

Andy cringed. "TMI, dude."

"You asked, fecker. Now hurry the hell up!"

Andy pointed his arm at the shark's gills and hoped the laser would nick something in the jaw to open them. It shifted a bit and he pressed the button for the laser. He sliced the head clean off in a single vertical swipe. The body twitched and bobbed for a moment before sinking.

"Eh," Sully said. "Little help here, boyo."

The goblin shark's head floated while the rest sank. Which Andy counted as a win. The last thing he wanted was to go any deeper for fear of killing Sully. They were already too deep. Still, the head did not sink. Sully writhed, trying to free himself from the clenched jaws.

"Hold on," Andy said. "I'm coming."

He boosted to Sully and the massive shark head. The slingshot jaws drooped without life and Sully dangled over the vast, dark abyss below. Then, the head began to sink.

Sully grunted and tried to pry the jaws open. He even slashed at the head with his laser. All to no avail. The problem was he faced the wrong direction. In order to make the laser effective, he'd have to twist his body almost one-hundred and eighty degrees. He stared down in the black water.

Andy glided to a stop at the sinking head. "Okay. Just hold still."

"I...ya need t'hurry. Can't...can't breathe very well, I can really feel 'er now."

Andy didn't say anything and cut into the crook of the goblin shark's jaw. Where the top met the bottom. That loosened everything a bit, though not enough. As Sully tried to pull himself free, Andy noted a couple of teeth snagged into the suit. He went to pull them free and stopped.

If the teeth penetrated the suit, that would mean more holes. Which also meant if Andy pulled the teeth out, more water would rush in. There was not a chance in hell Sully would make it. Once the teeth were out, he'd drown within seconds.

Heart stammering, Andy cut the teeth off the shark and pulled Sully free. Andy gave the Irishman a quick look over. There didn't appear to be any bubbles coming from around the severed teeth, so there was that.

The giant shark head slowly tumbled down into the dark depths of the Gulf of Mexico.

"A-Andy. Can't…can't breathe…"

Andy locked arms with Sully. "Tell your suit to rapid boost. We're going straight up."

"Rapid…b-boost…"

"Rapid boost," Andy said before Sully's suit shot off and dragged him helplessly behind.

It only took about a second to match Sully's speed. Andy aimed them at the surface, which was slightly lighter than all the rest. Barely lighter, though just enough. They blasted upward in a jet of bubbles.

"I…I can't…b-br…" Sully said.

"Just hold on," Andy said. "We're almost there."

Only about eighty feet to the surface, according to the visor.

"I…I can't…"

Another minute and they breached the surface in a spray of water. Andy rolled Sully over onto his back. "You need to tell the suit to open the visor."

"I…I…" He sounded like an overweight man trying to talk after a mile run. In other words, barely.

"You have to do it," Andy said, trying to control his own breathing. He ignored the fact that something very hungry could be lurking below them, ready to snap them up once and for all. Something so massive and frightening, it was beyond comparison.

Andy shook Sully. "You need to say it. Your visor won't recognize my voice."

Sully wheezed. "O…Open. V-Vis…" He coughed and Andy's heart sank.

"Try again," Andy said. He glanced around, taking in his surroundings on the surface for the first time.

To no surprise, there was nothing but bluish green water as far as the eye could see for miles. He held onto the Irishman while they bobbed through the mild waves. At least they were mild and not walls. They would probably be in tons of trouble if the surface was more turbulent.

They were not as close to shore as he thought. There wasn't any land to be seen. At all. Andy lowered his head and finally looked at Sully.

"You have to try again."

"Open...v-v-..."

Andy looked away. The man was going to die in his sui—

"Visor."

Sully's visor slipped open, revealing his freckled face. He sucked in a whoop of air. It took him a few seconds until he could breathe without trouble. His blue/green eyes flickered before finding Andy.

"What the...shit," Sully managed.

Andy smiled. "Ready to go see your kids?"

Sully glanced left and right. He scowled at the bright blue sky. "Better get movin' b'fore something down there decides t'snap us up, aye?"

Heart easing a bit, Andy nodded. "Right."

He thought about moving Sully around and holding him that way while they headed for shore, like a lifeguard saving a drowning victim. Instead, he positioned himself at the Irishman's side. If he went the lifeguard route, he wouldn't be able to see.

"Tell your suit to rapid boost," he told Sully. "On three."

"Okay. Ready, boyo."

"One. Two. Three."

They told their suits in unison to rapid boost and they were on their way toward whatever shore awaited them.

It burst out of the water like a nightmare beast through the dark pools of sleep about twenty yards ahead, a dolphin clutched in its jaws.

Sully and Andy slowed and stopped while the creature slammed back into the water and disappeared in waves of red.

"The feck was that?" Sully asked, blinking at the sky.

"I..." Andy frowned at the bloody waves. Blood surrounded them now. Blood everywhere. "Oh, shit. We need to go."

"What was it?" Sully asked. "White shark? Gobbie?"

"No." A shiver ran along Andy's spine. "I think it was a killer whale. Had a dolphin in its mouth."

Sully's eyes widened a bit more. "Feckin' orcas. There be any blood?"

"A lot."

"Aye. We need t'get movin'. Orcas are smart. They use the pod to fuck with their prey. Confuse and scare until the prey makes a stupid move. Then they tear it apart."

"Ready?" Andy asked. "High boost."

Sully said it only a second later, though it took everything Andy had to pull the man, so they matched speeds.

And that's when Andy looked behind them.

It came in like a giant torpedo just under the surface. It barreled in such a speed Andy feared the suits could not surpass. After a minute, or so, it continued to give chase, though fell back a few yards.

"Got one chasing us," Andy said as he tried to keep water from spraying onto the Irishman's face. To no avail, though. The poor man was getting drenched. Couldn't be helped right now.

"Best bet there be two more at our flanks. Maybe one right under us. They're plannin' an attack."

"I don't think our suits can outrun them."

"Nah. We need t'outsmart'em."

"How are we supposed to do that? If they have us pretty much surrounded, how are we going to beat them?"

"Aye, but we have one thing they don't."

Andy glanced at Sully. "What?"

The Irishman grinned. "Lasers."

It took Andy a few seconds for it to sink in. And, when it did, he nodded. "Okay."

His sight drifted to the orca tailing them like a sluggish torpedo.

CHAPTER 26

"Just shoot a hole in'er head," Sully said. "The rest will mourn'er and we'll get far enough away they'll forget.'

Andy frowned. "You sure? You said they were smart. What if they come after us for revenge?"

Sully shook his head, sputtered a bit from the sprays of water. He barely opened his eyes anymore. Probably because of how the saltwater sprayed into his face. Andy didn't blame him. That shit stung.

"Just shoot the fecker tailin' us. She's the leader."

Andy sighed and turned a bit to face the large orca following them. He couldn't make out a head or anything much due to all the water rolling off it, but he knew what needed to be done. Sully was right. Now, if he was right about the one following them being the leader or not…well…that was still up in the air.

Regardless, he pointed his arm at the torpedoing orca and pressed the button at the bottom of his palm. It was too light to see the laser itself, but he did notice the steam billowing from the water. The orca reared, toothy mouth opened wide. It made a loud shriek and dove below the surface.

"Hopefully she's dead'n y'didn't just piss'er off," Sully said.

"Well, shit," Andy said, "that makes me feel so much better."

Sully smiled. "That's m'boy."

"I wasn't serious."

Sully chuckled. "And that's the beauty of it."

Andy frowned at the Irishman, not sure how to react, though smiling despite himself. Their speed through the warm waters of the Gulf never slowed.

"Best to keep movin' too. Stay this speed. Just in case she's still alive and comin' up with a new plan."

"Right," Andy said, sparing a glance behind them again.

The water wasn't black. It glistened and shimmered, rolling under the hot sun. Quite spectacularly beautiful. Made you fall into deep lapses of cold drinks and palm trees. Of inviting music and long, white beaches.

Ah, but it was only the surface. Like most surfaces, it was gorgeous and welcoming. Why, it almost purred, "Come on in. The water is fine." Below it, however, darkness waited. The deeper you went, the darker it got until there was nothing but black water, and the horrors which lurked within it. Things that would bite. Ravenous things. Giant things. Monsters…

Andy shivered and returned his gaze to the north.

Eventually, they found land.

CHAPTER 27

The beach they scraped up on wasn't white, but a light tan.

Not Florida, then.

It was also deserted.

Andy opened his visor and stood on wobbly legs. It was like they forgot how to work for a few seconds. Too much time in the water did that. He just forgot about that little tid-bit. The air was hot and sticky to his skin and salty when he opened his mouth to ask Sully if he was alright.

"Other than feelin' waterlogged...aye, I'm okay."

Andy exited his suit and was helping Sully get out of his when he noticed the man's leg. A lone seagull shrieked at them. A mild wind blew off the water. For a moment, neither man said anything until Andy went to sit Sully down on the beach.

"Best get m'to a hospital. Startin' to hurt."

Andy nodded. "Okay." He slung Sully's arm over his shoulders so he could better help the man. "I don't know where we are, though."

Sully winced in apparent pain with every movement. The leg itself oozed a mixture of blood and yellowish pus. A tooth broke the skin and being submerged and stuck in salt water for hours made the wound worse than it should have been. Or, at least, that's what Andy thought. For all he knew, the goblin sharks had some kind of bacteria or venom.

"Jus' keep walkin' boyo," Sully said, partially through gritted teeth. "Gotta be a road."

Andy glanced ahead once they mounted the sand dune away from the beach, and his heart sank. For as far as he could see there was nothing but desert.

Sully grunted. "Must be Texas."

Andy held Sully up as best as he could and began their trek into the hot wastelands before them.

***

He wasn't sure how long they'd been shuffling along before Sully began to convulse.

The Irishman managed, "Shit," and seized against Andy.

Using all his strength to keep the man from flopping around like a dying fish, Andy held Sully down. The sun seared into the top of his head and back of his neck. Yellow foam spewed from Sully's mouth. All Andy could find strength enough to do was gape at his friend.

Oh, god. What do I? What do I do? What do I—

A hot wind blew at his back. Mellow humming replaced the dead silence of the desert.

You're imagining that, he thought. *You're thirsty. You're delusional. Nothing—*

"Andy?"

The voice, it was familiar, but, for the life of him, he couldn't put a face to it.

Two men in black tactical gear dropped to their knees at the head and feet of Sully. One of them, no older than thirty, shot a glance at Andy.

"Get inside. We'll take care of him."

Andy blinked and stood on legs that might as well have been pillars of gelatin. Get inside where, though? He swayed and strong hands steadied him.

"Got ya, pal," a man said. "Let's hydrate, yeah?"

Andy managed a weak nod and let himself be led to something that appeared to be a large hovercraft. He barely made it up the ladder to an open door. He shivered from the cool air drifting out of the doorway.

Then the face to the familiar voice emerged from inside the hovercraft. A face full of concern.

"Oh, Andy," Angela Wexler said, helping him inside. "I'm so sorry."

He sat down in a soft cushioned seat and drank some water while someone else pulled a cool blanket over him.

In his ear, Wexler said, "It'll be okay, Andy. It'll be okay now."

THREE MONTHS LATER

"Ready?" Andy readied his M4 carbine.

"No," Sully said. "But feck it. We came this far, aye?"

Andy smiled, nodded. "Aye."

Sully, thankfully, didn't lose the leg. Though the venom from the goblin shark's bite about killed him. Luckily Wexler had tracking devices in their suits as well as the minisub. She knew where they were the entire time, though, according to her, couldn't send anyone to help. Andy didn't believe her fully on that. Nor did he believe they were saved from the desert because she cared about them.

Sully was used to extract the venom in his blood. Which, they both found out later, would go on to help treat, or even cure some cancers.

All that made it hard to be mad at the woman. In the end, they saved lives anyway.

As for the massive goblin sharks in the tunnels below the Gulf of Mexico, he didn't know. Wexler was mute on the subject, no matter how much he tried. And he didn't try too much because she paid him now. She gave him the life he dreamed of. Simple, bringing in good money for his kids to live well.

Andy armed sweat away from his eyes. He stood at one side of large double doors while Sully stood on the other. Nearby were two dead guards, both with holes in their foreheads.

What they were about to do, though, it was for Wexler.

No.

This was for the hell they had to endure in the tunnels.

This was for free...

"Now," Andy whispered and kicked open the double doors.

Carlito Guerra rose from his chair, pistol in hand. "¿Quién carajo eres tú?"

Andy knew enough Spanish to somewhat understand the question: "Who the fuck are you?"

Sully cut down two more guards while Andy slowly advanced.

He glared at the drug lord. "Venganza." Vengeance.

Guerra's eyes widened. He pointed the pistol at Andy.

Andy side stepped, aim still trained on the drug lord, and squeezed the trigger of his M4.

Kings will fall.

Castles will crumble.

Justice will be served.

THE END

CHECK OUT OTHER GREAT DEEP SEA THRILLERS

THE BREACH
by Edward J. McFadden III

A Category 4 hurricane punched a quarter mile hole in Fire Island, exposing the Great South Bay to the ferocity of the Atlantic Ocean, and the current pulled something terrible through the new breach. A monstrosity of the past mixed with the present has been disturbed and it's found its way into the sheltered waters of Long Island's southern sea.

Nate Tanner lives in Stones Throw, Long Island. A disgraced SCPD detective lieutenant put out to pasture in the marine division because of his Navy background and experience with aquatic crime scenes, Tanner is assigned to hunt the creeper in the bay. But he and his team soon discover they're the ones being hunted.

INFESTATION
by William Meikle

It was supposed to be a simple mission. A suspected Russian spy boat is in trouble in Canadian waters. Investigate and report are the orders.

But when Captain John Banks and his squad arrive, it is to find an empty vessel, and a scene of bloody mayhem.

Soon they are in a fight for their lives, for there are things in the icy seas off Baffin Island, scuttling, hungry things with a taste for human flesh.

They are swarming. And they are growing.

"Scotland's best Horror writer" - Ginger Nuts of Horror

"The premier storyteller of our time." - Famous Monsters of Filmland

 SEVEREDPRESS

𝕏 twitter.com/severedpress

CHECK OUT OTHER GREAT
DEEP SEA THRILLERS

SHARK: INFESTED WATERS
by P.K. Hawkins

For Simon, the trip was supposed to be a once in a lifetime gift: a journey to the Amazon River Basin, the land that he had dreamed about visiting since he was a child. His enthusiasm for the trip may be tempered by the poor conditions of the boat and their captain leading the tour, but most of the tourists think they can look the other way on it. Except things go wrong quickly. After a horrific accident, Simon and the other tourists find themselves trapped on a tiny island in the middle of the river. It's the rainy season, and the river is rising. The island is surrounded by hungry bull sharks that won't let them swim away. And worst of all, the sharks might not be the only blood-thirsty killers among them. It was supposed to be the trip of a lifetime. Instead, they'll be lucky if they make it out with their lives at all.

DARK WATERS
by Lucas Pederson

Jörmungandr is an ancient Norse sea monster. Thought to be purely a myth until a battleship is torn a part by one.

With his brother on that ship, former Navy Seal and deep-sea diver, Miles Raine, sets out on a personal vendetta against the creature and hopefully save his brother. Bringing with him his old Seal team, the Dagger Points, they embark on a mission that might very well be their last.

But what happens when the hunters become the hunted and the dark waters reveal more than a monster?

CHECK OUT OTHER GREAT DEEP SEA THRILLERS

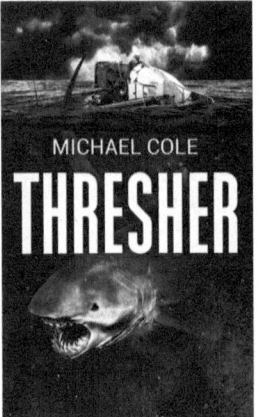

THRESHER
by Michael Cole

In the aftermath of a hurricane, a series of strange events plague the coastal waters off Florida. People go into the water and never return. Corpses of killer whales drift ashore, ravaged from enormous bite marks. A fishing trawler is found adrift, with a mysterious gash in its hull.

Transferred to the coastal town of Merit, police officer Leonard Riker uncovers the horrible reality of an enormous Thresher shark lurking off the coast. Forty feet in length, it has taken a territorial claim to the waters near the town harbor. Armed with three-inch teeth, a scythe-like caudal fin, and unmatched aggression, the beast seeks to kill anything sharing the waters.

THE GUILLOTINE
by Lucas Pederson

1,000 feet under the surface, Prehistoric Anthropologist, Ash Barrington, and his team are in the midst of a great archeological dig at the bottom of Lake Superior where they find a treasure trove of bones. Bones of dinosaurs that aren't supposed to be in this particular region. In their underwater facility, Infinity Moon, Ash and his team soon discover a series of underground tunnels. Upon exploring, they accidentally open an ice pocket, thawing the prehistoric creature trapped inside. Soon they are being attacked, the facility falling apart around them, by what Ash knows is a dunkleosteus and all those bones were from its prey. Now...Ash and his team are the prey and the creature will stop at nothing to get to them.